Murder  **Kingdom**

Text Copyright © 2013 Andrew Drummond

All rights reserved

To Jean; for her love, kindness and never ending support

Preface

Welcome to the Age of Gold, a period of Egyptian history that lasted approximately 400 years. It started almost a thousand years after the last of the great pyramids of Ghiza was built. The Age of Gold coincided with the rise and fall of the New Kingdom dynasties of Theban Pharaohs. It lasted from BC 1539 to the end of the 11th Century BC. At its zenith, foreign princes believed that gold was as plentiful in Egypt as the country's desert sands were. They wrote begging letters to the Pharaohs, asking to be sent ships full of gold, as if they were offering to take unwanted rubbish off their hands! But gold held a special significance for the Egyptian people of the New Kingdom. Because of the metal's shiny, sun like appearance, they believed it to be the very flesh of the gods. And not just of any god, but their most revered god – Amun-Re. He was the King of all gods and the manifestation of the sun, who lived in the sacred Temple at Karnak. They believed that the sun rose everyday, only because Amun-Re had sailed his golden Barque into the underworld, where he accompanied and then retrieved the golden disc from darkness.

The New Kingdom comprised of three dynasties; the 18th, 19th and 20th. Throughout their reigns gold was not always in plentiful supply. It certainly was not at the very start of the 18th Dynasty, when the Hyksos ruled Upper Egypt. They were a mixed Semitic and Asian race, who came out of Canaan to conquer the Nile delta. For more than a hundred years they held sway over Northern Egypt. During the 19th Dynasty, apart from the reign of Ramesses II, or Great, Egypt did not have vast amounts of wealth at its disposal. And the 20th Dynasty was so impoverished that it instituted official tomb robbing to top up the administration's treasury. The last

Pharaoh of that dynasty, Ramesses XI, was petrified that his tomb would be robbed after his burial. He was so afraid that he moved the centre of government out of Thebes, which meant that he would not have to be buried in the Valley of Kings.

But physical evidence of the plentiful Age of Gold was provided in 1922, when Howard Carter uncovered the tomb of Tutankhamun in the Valley of the Kings. He uncovered golden treasures that have continued to astound the world, by their opulence and beauty, ever since. The discovery made Tutankhamun into the most famous Egyptian Pharaoh in the world. Although the truth was rather different, because he was a relatively insignificant figure in Egyptian history. Even his burial place is unspectacular, being a small, four roomed tomb. He died before he reached the age of eighteen. So his entire reign of nine years was spent as a minor, under the influence of mature advisers. Tutankhamun had no chance to stamp his own mark on Egypt. It was left to his funerary offerings to do that for him.

The size of the gold hoard that he was buried with poses two very important questions. The first is why did the Egyptians bury massive amounts of gold with their Kings – even with a minor Pharaoh? To answer that, we must return to their belief that gold was the flesh or skin of the gods. Gold would ensure eternal life for the departed monarch. It would hasten his assimilation into the sun, so that he could become one with Amun-Re. The second question posed is a more practical and geographical one. Where did Egypt get such amounts of gold, that foreign potentates believed it to be as plentiful as sand? It was obtained from Nubia, or modern day Sudan – but only after the conquering Hyksos had been defeated.

Nubia lay to the south of Egypt and the Hyksos' stronghold was to its north. The Hyksos invasion had split Egypt in two. Egyptian resistance was centred around Thebes, or Waset, as it was then known. Eventually the Theban princes rose up in revolt and after several abortive attempts overthrew their conquerors. The last King of the 17th Dynasty, Khamose, started the campaign. But the final victory came under Amose I, who was the founder of the 18th Dynasty. With its northern borders secured Egypt was now able to turn her attention south – towards Nubia and the Kingdom of Kush. The Nubian goldmines contained massive reserves of gold. Unfortunately for them, the southern neighbours had responded to overtures by the Hyksos, when the war was turning in favour of Egypt. Although it took 30 years, until the reign of Tuthmosis I, Kush and Nubia were finally conquered and subdued. Egypt now had Nubian gold to add to its own resources. These were mined at Wadi Hammamat, in the desert to the east of the Nile Valley.

Following the reign of Tuthmosis III, the Pharaohs of the 18th Dynasty consolidated Egypt's wealth. Although the gold was important, it was not the only source of the country's prosperity. Under Amenhotep III Egypt expanded her influence abroad. Egypt had grain, wine and other food produce in profusion. There is historical evidence of increased trade links across the Mediterranean. From this period on, we find Egyptian artefacts appearing in mainland Greece and vice versa. Amenhotep III ruled Egypt firmly and wisely for almost 40 years. He left behind a Kingdom that was unified and wealthy. Its southern and northern borders were secure. Internationally, Egypt had trading partners from Minoa, the greatest sea borne power of the day, to Mycenae on the Greek mainland. But then everything started to go horribly wrong.

It is against that background that this novel is set, towards the end of the 18th dynasty. Egypt was living in the peaceful and prosperous Age of Gold. But a new Pharaoh had recently ascended to the throne. He was Amenhotep IV, the son of Amenhotep III and the 10th King of the 18th dynasty. His wife is reputed to be one of the most desirable women who have ever lived. Her name is Nefertiti, which means, "The beautiful one has arrived". But neither will keep their names for much longer, as they soon rename themselves. Amenhotep IV will also be renamed by his subjects and history as "The Heretic Pharaoh". Egyptian society and its institutions will crumble and fall. The Age of Gold will turn into an age of turmoil and strife.

The story is told through the eyes of Nakht, a soldier in the King's army. It starts ten years after Amenhotep IV's death. Nakht is in command of a special mission. His force is waiting in a desert. They are two days' chariot ride from the shifting border, in the part of modern Syria that was then controlled by Egypt. Over recent years, the Egyptian empire's northern frontier has been eroded and pushed back. Further north, across the border is the part of Syria that is ruled by the Hittites. They originate from modern day Turkey. Their southern base and stronghold is on the other side of the river Euphrates. Now that the Hyksos have been vanquished, the Hittites are the new northern menace to the safety of Upper Egypt. But as Nakht is about to painfully discover, neither the present or even the future can be easily unravelled from the past.

Chapter One

Zannanza, the young Hittite prince from Anatolia, died screaming for mercy as Nakht slit his throat. The sharp, bronze blade sliced through his flesh and windpipe with the minimum of effort. It helped that Nakht's men were holding the man down. So all the Commander had to do was tug the man's hair backwards and apply the finishing blow. While Zannanza choked on his own blood and gurgled for breath the soldiers released him, to writhe in the sand. Nakht also relaxed his grip and watched, almost dispassionately, as the Hittite's lifeblood spurted out onto the desert sand. It wasn't the first murder that he had committed for the state. And he was more than sure that it was by no means going to be the last. As the prince's corpse suddenly stopped its convulsions and fell silent, Nakht said to his second in command Djar, "I'm sure that King Suppiliulamas had no idea that we would be waiting for his son. Now, do your duty and cut off his right hand. And make sure that the royal ring stays on his finger. Lord Ay intends to make a present of both to his new sweetheart..."

Djar grunted his acknowledgement at his superior's instructions and drew his curved sword. One of the men placed a small rock underneath the base of the deceased prince's wrist. Djar raised his sword and brought it down in one swift motion, lopping off the dead man's hand. With the job done, the second soldier needed no bidding. He retrieved the severed hand and wrapped it tightly in a linen bandage. Turning to his Commander, Djar said, "I take it we'll be leaving the rest of him for the birds or wild animals, sir?"

"You are correct in that assumption. The sooner we are away from here the better. Get the men ready to move out, after they have drunk from the Hittites' water skins."

"Shall I get you some water to drink, Commander?"

Nakht shook his head and walked back to the rocky outcrop without replying verbally. There would be time for him to drink when they rejoined the chariots.

The ambush had gone according to plan. They had left their own chariots in an oasis five miles away, the horses tethered and under guard. Nakht and Djar had then marched their force of twenty men through the desert to the rocky outcrop. That way there had been no chance of their horses alerting the Hittite party. Under his command he had Djar, ten archers and ten swordsmen. They had all concealed themselves and waited many hours for the Hittites to arrive. He had forbidden his men to bring any water with them, as he did not want any distractions. The waiting had been thirsty work. But their discipline and attention had held. Eventually the Hittites had arrived. It had been easy for the Egyptians to pick out the prince, as the rest of his entourage were obviously soldiers, like themselves. The Commander had let the party ride into bow range. At his signal, the archers had unleashed several volleys, at the horses and the men. The Hittites had been taken by complete surprise and several of their chariots had overturned. After his archers had loosed off two more strings of arrows, he had led the charge down the rocky outcrop. Falling upon the disoriented enemy their swords had quickly finished the job that the arrows had started.

Before the ambush Nakht had given strict instructions that the prince be brought to him alive. Four of his men had carried the struggling, young man from his upturned chariot and presented him to their superior officer. Although Nakht did not speak the language of the Hittites, he did have a cuneiform tablet that Lord Ay had provided. Exactly how, or from whom, Ay had obtained it, the officer had known better than to ask. He held the hardened clay rectangle up in front of Zannanza. The prince's light brown face had immediately turned white. Then his eyes had started to roll around his skull, as he glanced down at the wedge shaped writing. The look of recognition on his face, spoke far greater volumes than the Hittite gibberish streaming from his mouth. But just to be sure, Nakht pointed directly at him and said one word, "Ankesenamun."

Zannanza had then proved that "no" was universally understood in any language, with a loud howl and several shakes of his head. But it was his last meaningful act on this earth. Nakht had replaced the cuneiform tablet, in the pouch hanging from his kilt and signalled for his men to hold the prince down, before slicing through his windpipe. Job done, he thought to himself, as he sat on the on the rocky outcrop alone. waiting impatiently for his men to finish drinking the Hittites' water. The sun was starting to dip westwards and he wanted to reach the chariots before dusk fell. Nakht was no longer a young man, being almost forty years of age. Many of his countrymen did not live beyond that age. He was, however, a supremely fit and hardened man. A lifetime of military service in a crack unit had stood his body in good stead. The soldier was also a tall man, fully two hands higher than most, if not all, of his contemporaries. When the men rejoined him on the outcrop, he inclined his head towards the sun. Then he pointed at the tracks that they had earlier made in the sand and said, "Rather than walk we will run at a slow pace to the chariots. Time is short."

Without any further instructions, he led off and the men followed in his wake. The soldiers realised that their leader had spoken the truth about night being close. They also knew that he had not drunk any of the Hittites' water. So it was their duty and a point of honour to keep up with the pace that he set. As always Djar ran two paces behind him. Like the rest of the men, he had the utmost respect for their Commander. Although this respect was tinged with feelings of fear. Not one of the soldiers knew where Nakht got his strength and energy from. In the barracks it was commonly held that he cast daily spells in the name of Montu, the war god. Some men even went as far as to claim that he was not human in the first place. But they tended to be the ones who had failed the exacting standards that Nakht expected and usually received from troops under his command.

The journey back to the chariots seemed to take the men forever. Two or three had almost become detached from the main group. It was as well that they could only see the back of Nakht's head, because he was smiling at their discomfort. Not because he was a sadist, which he wasn't. But because they had filled their bellies with water. The return journey to the chariots had been his reason for not drinking. Of course, he had been as thirsty as any of the men. But he knew that they would have to jog on the return journey. And he did not want his belly flopping up and down, as his feet contended with the strength, sapping sand. Breathing in deeply, he shouted behind to Djar, "Have the men keep the pace. I want no stragglers."

His second in command did not need to issue any order. The soldiers had heard his voice and swiftly bunched together again on Djar's shoulder. Although it did take the potential stragglers a short time to catch up with their fitter comrades.

Eventually, they reached the oasis where they had concealed their chariots. Moreys and Amptu were the two soldiers who had been left in charge of the vehicles. They were glad to see their comrades return without any casualties. There was an unspoken law in the barracks that Nakht always brought back as many men as he took out. The two soldiers who had remained behind swiftly offered everyone water. While Nakht was quenching his thirst, they prepared a supper of bread, which was served with dried meat and dried fruits. The ravenous detail devoured it, as if they were eating the finest delicacies in the whole of Egypt, which even the King would be pleased to see it on his table. When they had all eaten and drunk their fill, Nakht went over to his chariot, leaving the men to chatter amongst themselves. He took up a thick linen blanket and wrapped it around himself. The Commander also took up the remnants of a once full skin of wine. There was no need for him to organise a guard detail. Moreys and Amptu knew that was their job, as they had remained behind in charge of the detail's chariots.

Nakht scraped out a hollow in the sand to accommodate his torso and legs. He then stretched out, into the soft sand and rested his tired body. Next he did what he always did after carrying out a murder for Ay. He drank heavily from the wine skin. Sleep was out of the question. It never came easily, and sometimes never came at all, after a killing. So he closed his eyes and thought back to his childhood, *when as a small boy the only ambition he had was to become a scribe...*

Chapter Two

..Nakht had grown up in a small village, called Bathar, which was situated on one of the seven tributaries, which flowed through the Nile Delta. From his village it took four days' journey in a boat to travel upriver to Thebes. Of course, as a small child he had no real conception of any place other than Bathar. To him the outside world was where his father sometimes went, in the season of Peret, after the crops had been planted. It seemed that the King always needed his help, at that time in particular, to build some new houses. The boy's world revolved around the fields and the marshes surrounding Bathar. His father was called Hapu. Like the other men of the village he farmed barley, wheat and vegetables in land that had been reclaimed from the river. When they were not farming the land, they fished the river and tended the papyrus beds in the nearby marshes. It was a poor community where families rarely ate meat, other than wildfowl or fish. But nobody starved, even though most families had many small mouths to feed. And because of the barley, the older children and their parents had plenty of beer to drink.

In many ways, it had been a carefree and untroubled upbringing. The smaller children wandered around naked, as did some of the fishermen. There were always games to play, especially when the river flooded and there was no work to be done in the fields. In the hot summer, those men who dressed wore only a small apron or loincloth. This was to keep the sun off that most delicate parts of their bodies. The women of the village tended to wear rough linen tunics, which came down to their knees. They spent more time indoors or under shade than their men folk, so their skin was not so resistant to the strong heat of the sun.

Although Nakht's father did own a short linen kilt, which he kept for special occasions. But Hapu only wore it when attending religious festivals at the local temple. Other than that, it just saw service when the royal officials, papyrus dealers or a scribe visited their small village.

Bathar was no different to any of the thousands of settlements dotted along the length of the river Nile. Children went out to work with their fathers, as soon as they were tall enough to be useful. In Nakht's case, because of his size, this was from an early age. So he spent a lot of time listening to his father, as they worked the fields together. He became a lot closer to him than he was to his mother, Ese. Hapu was not an educated man, but he was an intelligent man. Very few Egyptians, who were outside the elite classes, were literate or numerate and his father was no exception. But as Nakht grew older he realised that his father had a brain and was not afraid to use it. He also started to understand more and more of the older man's conversation. Especially when he talked about the wonderful life that a scribe enjoyed and the houses that his father, and those before him, had helped the Pharaoh build. His father also told him about the wonderful life that a scribe enjoyed. An educated man, he told his son, who was always guaranteed a living.

Nakht had to wait until he was almost eight years old before he met a scribe, in person. Although, he had previously seen several of them pass through the village. But just before his eighth birthday, an itinerant scribe called into Bathar. It was shortly after harvest time, in the season of Shemu, and followed after the visit of the royal officials. The officials were always followed closely by the papyrus dealers. By their own standards, the villagers were now well off – so the scribe knew that there would be a market for his services. He opened his bundle and set up his stool, in the shade of a tree, before laying out the tools of his profession. Then he sat there and waited, until one by one, men from the village approached him. Hapu was one of his first customers, having changed into his linen kilt as soon as he saw the man arrive. In the past, he had left his eldest son with the other children, while he conducted his business. But on this occasion, he had decided that it was time for the boy to learn about another world. The one that existed far outside the constricted confines of Bathar.

As one of his neighbours made barter payment to the scribe and left carrying a small piece of papyrus, Hapu approached the visitor. Nakht stood silently by his father's side. The scribe looked up at the pair of them and said,
"And just how may I help you, my good man and young lad?"

"I need two spells to be written down, if it pleases your excellency," Hapu answered, the tone in his voice respectful.

"Ah yes," was the scribe's haughty reply, after a moment's hesitation, "I had expected you to ask for spells. Out in the delta villages there is no call for any other form of writing. No wills or letters to relatives. Just spells..."

Nakht could sense that his father wanted to say something, but seemed to think better of it. When Hapu eventually responded he said "One is for our Lord Amun. I want to ask him to ensure that the delta floods well during the next inundation, during the season of Akhet. And the second is to Shay, for my boy here, Nakht. I want him to grow up to be a healthy and prosperous man, who enjoys a long life."

"Very sensible too, on both counts. Did you know that your boy's name means "The Strong One?" I'm more than sure that you did. Now, bear with me please, your spells will only take me a couple of minutes," the scribe said, as he took up two tiny, rectangles of papyrus. He then dipped his pen into the ink, which he had made up from water and lamp black. The father and son watched with fascination as the man's quill pen scratched across the surface of the first piece of papyrus. Slowly the hieroglyphs took shape, conferring an importance and meaning on the previously blank surface. "This is the spell for Amun," he told them, before placing the first rectangle to dry in the sun. Then the scribe, a kindly looking man who was many years older than the boy's father, smiled at Nakht and said, "Before I start on the one for your lad, good sir, may I ask if any of your neighbours have been annoying you?"

"No more than usual," Hapu responded, obviously puzzled by the enquiry.

"Fair enough," the scribe answered, "But I am in possession of a very powerful excretory spell. It was recently given to me by a senior priest from the temple at Heliopolis. Why, only four villages away from here, it turned a man's nose into a donkey's snout and an enormous hairy tail grew out of his arse!"

Nakht was entranced by the visitor's words and hoped that his father had not upset any body in the village. He doubted that he could bear the shame of seeing his father walking around the community with a donkey's snout in place of a own nose and a huge tail hanging down from his arse. Hapu on the other hand, being older, seemed less convinced of the veracity of this story. Less convinced maybe, but not totally disbelieving. Like all Egyptians, high or low, he had an unfaltering belief in the power of magic. There was not a man or woman in the village who didn't have a roughly, carved pendant suspended from their necks. The older man swallowed slightly nervously and said to the scribe, "I...I'll just take the one for the boy, thank you. Next time maybe, excellency, if I need the excretory spell, that is..." Nakht could see that his father was slightly unbalanced by the scribe's offer. Although he was young and inexperienced, the boy could sense some sort of immense power in the pen and fingertips of the old man. That made him realise why his father was so envious of the scribe's profession.

Meanwhile the old scribe had lowered his head and returned to penning Nakht's spell. As he formed the hieroglyphs Hapu said, "Forgive me for interrupting your work, Master, but I can't help noticing that you are not as young as you used to be. Maybe you have thought of taking an apprentice? A strong, young lad who could carry your things and look out for you...a youngster who would be keen to learn. Like my boy, here..."

"It is kind of you to ask," the scribe responded, without raising his head, "But I have sons and grand sons aplenty at home. When the time comes, they'll look after their old man. I'm sure of that. But please, don't give up hope for your boy. As strange as it may seem there was a famous scribe of the same name who worked for our Pharaoh. I believe that he died only recently."

Nakht looked up and saw his father bite his bottom lip at this reply. An expression of disappointment also rippled across Hapu's face. This was unseen by the scribe who was putting the finishing touches to the second spell. When it was complete, the scribe put it to dry on the ground, alongside the incantation to Amun. Hapu then made payment for the two small rectangles of papyrus. The scribe handed him the first spell and said, "Tie this one around your pendant the next time you visit the river, to fish. Once the ink is washed away the magic will enter the water and flow down to the great sea. As for your boy, well, I suppose you must know that he has to drink his spell to Shay."

It was Nakht's turn to look perplexed. But his father placed a reassuring arm on his boy's shoulder and said to him, "Don't worry son. It's nothing at all to worry about, just the opposite in fact. No harm at all will come to you. I'll show you what to do after we have eaten this evening." The scribe then handed the second spell to Hapu and bade them both a curt good day. The old man's next customer took their place almost instantly and impatiently.

That night, after the family had eaten, Hapu consecrated the spell to Amun. The farmer knelt and prayed in front of the small family shrine, at the rear of their living room. Then he took his oldest son to the fields. He also took a large container of beer and a smaller vessel filled with water. Nakht was feeling very apprehensive - but at the same time quite interested. The father and son sat down together on a piece of raised ground. Hapu placed the small vessel filled with water in front of the boy, before saying to him, "For the spell to work you must drink the ink from the papyrus. Here – watch!"

In the moonlight, he saw his father place the rectangle of papyrus face down into the water. Using his forefinger Hapu pressed it down several times. Then he picked up the beaker and swirled the contents round. Finally he removed the now blank papyrus and handed the vessel to his son, saying,

"Dedicate yourself to Shay and drink this down in one. It may taste strange, but we have plenty of beer to wash away any after taste."

Following his father's instructions, the boy swallowed the water and forced it to stay down. Mentally, he pledged himself to the god of fate, feeling quite important and grown up, now that he had his own personal god. When Hapu saw that he had finished the liquid he poured some beer into the beaker and said, "Drink that, but not all at once. You might find it to have a funny taste, but you'd better get used to it. You are becoming quite a big man now."

In the delta, just as in the rest of Egypt, beer was an integral part of most people's diet. Feeling even more grown up, Nakht raised the vessel to his lips and sipped at the cloudy brown liquid. His father was right. It did have a funny taste – if anything it was worse than the spell water. Hapu smiled happily at his son's expression and said, "I'm sure that you can see now, why I am always talking to you about the life that a scribe leads. All that power and knowledge in one man..."

"Yes, father, it must be wonderful to make magic spells."

But Hapu shook his head in disappointment at his son's words. He thought for a moment before saying, "No, boy. That wasn't what I meant. To begin with, the scribe doesn't cast the spells. That is the job of the priests in the temples. A scribe just copies them out and sells them to the likes of us. And that's just one way that he makes a living."

"I thought you said that he had power and knowledge, father..."

"He does, but only because he can read and write. We can't and nobody will teach us. Look at his reply when I asked if he wanted an apprentice. He said that he had sons and grandsons. Well, I'm sure they can all read and write and are doing very nicely out of it."

As Hapu's voice tailed off, his son considered the older man's words. Then he took another sip of the cloudy beer and said, "Father, I think that I can see what you mean. I noticed that the scribe had very smooth hands. A man of his age should have rough and wrinkled skin on his hands."

"Clever boy, you're beginning to understand. A scribe does not have to farm or fish to eat. All he has to do is write. But it's not just his hands that make him different to us. Did you notice his kilt and footwear?"

"I did," Nakht replied, "The kilt was long and pleated. It was smooth and came down to below his knees. And his sandals were made of strong leather."

"Such materials are not cheap. I would imagine that he probably has several such kilts and pairs of sandals. But there is another thing for you to remember. If you or I walk to the next village or the nearest town, we are not even guaranteed a welcome. He is guaranteed an income or food and drink wherever he goes. And it's all because there are so few people that can read and write!"

It was at that moment that Nakht decided that he was going to be a scribe. He would become the first person from Bathar to learn how to read and write the sacred hieroglyphs. Then he could travel up and down the river. In time he would become a wealthy man, wearing a long linen kilt and sturdy footwear. The boy grinned at his father and took another draught of his beer. Its taste was starting to improve and the grin soon turned into a giggle. By the time he had finished several beakers of the liquid, Nakht was starting to feel quite sleepy. Above his head the stars were circling in a strange circular motion. His father noticed the effect that the beer was having on the boy. He finished his own drink and with a bit of difficulty, took Nakht up, into his strong arms, saying "Come on, lad. We should be getting back now. I think you are more than ready to sleep."

Nakht was half asleep, but he could still make out his father's words. So he answered, "When I am a scribe, dad, I'll send half of my earnings home. My family will be the richest in the village and nobody will dare to curse you with a donkey's snout and tail."

Unlike his mini hangover the following day, Nakht's dream never went away. Each year, whenever a scribe visited the village he was always at the front of the queue, along with his father. It wasn't always the same scribe that appeared. Indeed the old scribe, from that memorable day in his young life, was never seen again in Bathar. On each occasion the pair went through the same ritual. One spell for Amun and one for Shay. And whenever Hapu slipped in the question about a possible apprenticeship for his son, the answer was always the same. A polite no. But the boy refused to be discouraged, as he knew that it was his destiny. Besides, over the four years that followed he learnt a great deal from Hapu, as they worked alongside each other. His father told him about the Pharaoh, who saved Egypt from chaos by interceding with the gods. He also learnt that Amun was the most powerful and revered of all the deities. Four days away from Bathar there were massive houses called temples, where Amun lived in the afterlife and was tended to by his servants. And finally he learnt about some mysterious buildings, called pyramids, which were taller than many mountains. They could be seen on the way to Amun's house, but his father had no idea who had built them or for what reason they had been constructed. They were just pyramids and had to be accepted as such, his father told him.

Then one day, just after his twelfth birthday came the meeting that changed his life. It was the season of Shemu again. Their crops had already been harvested, so other than fishing and hunting wild fowl, there was not much work for the children to do. The scribe and papyrus dealers had made their annual visits. Nakht had been playing with his brothers and sisters, in front of their mud bricked house when a stranger rode into the village. His appearance caused the whole community came to an abrupt halt, because he was stood on a sort of woven chair, with wheels, which was being pulled by two horses. The youth quickly realised, from what his father had told him, that the visitor was a very important man. Although he had never seen such a vehicle, he knew that the stranger was driving a chariot. His mouth dropped as he looked at him and noted his long kilt and the strip of linen that he was wearing around his shoulders. But it wasn't only his clothes and chariot that marked the man out. He also had a full head of dark human hair. All of the people in the village kept their heads shaved, because of the bugs that liked to live in human hair.

Nakht's stomach suddenly started to churn with excitement. This visitor could only be the Chief Scribe to the whole of Egypt, if he was rich enough to own two horses and a chariot. Leaving his brothers and sisters, Nakht grabbed a jug of water and ran over to the vehicle. To his mind, it was obvious that the dignitary had been told about him. His servants must have said that there was a boy in this village worth recruiting to be a scribe. So, he must have sought out Bathar to find him, Nakht. He was going to be a scribe after all! When the boy reached the chariot, which had pulled up, he offered the jug to the Chief Scribe saying, "Lordship, I thought that you might be thirsty, sir. Please take it – the water is clean...and it's fresh too. I drew it from the well just after the sun had reached its mid point!"

The charioteer looked the almost naked boy up and down. He was a short man and around the same age as Nakht's father. After taking the jug from the youth he wiped his brow and said, "I thank you, young man that's very kind of you. Now tell me something.

Do you know where exactly we are, because I certainly do not? I was out in the delta hunting wildfowl and got myself separated from the others in my party."

Nakht's stomach sank and his initial excitement evaporated immediately. If the Chief Scribe had got lost hunting, then he had certainly not come to find him. Masking his disappointment, as best as he could, he answered, "You are in Bathar, Lordship. By boat, we are four days away from Amun's house, which my father helps the King to build, when he is needed…"

The stranger let out a loud guffaw of laughter and nearly choked on the mouthful of water that he was swallowing. When he had recovered he said, "I know where Karnak is, lad. But where in the Pharaoh's name is Bathar?"

Behind him, Nakht could hear the villagers sniggering at his discomfort. In the boy's opinion they were only too ready to see somebody take a fall – and derive pleasure from it. Fortunately, his father appeared at his shoulder and after bowing to the charioteer explained where he might find his colleagues. And that could have been it, until the stranger realised that he still had Nakht's pitcher in his chariot. He called the youth over to return the clay vessel and at the same time said to Hapu, "I take it that he is your son, farmer. Well, he is a credit to you. Hospitality, humour and geography are not often found in one sentence. How old is he?"

"He is just turned twelve, Lord…and he hopes to train for a scribe. He's a very bright and ambitious lad."

Nakht felt very embarrassed at these words of praise, after his earlier misconception. Although this time the visitor did not laugh at his father. Instead he replied, "Ambition, eh? I like that. And the boy could pass for fourteen, if not older. But a scribe, no. With his size and strength he could better serve the Pharaoh as a soldier, like myself."

Both the father and son's ears pricked up. The rest of the village had stopped their snide mutterings and were now listening intently. Hapu asked, "And who might you be, Lord?"

"My name is Ay and I am not yet a Lord, but a mere captain in our King's personal guard. Now, for two bars of gold, I'll take this boy off your hands and teach him a man's trade. But he will be allowed to learn how to read and write, if he really wants that sort of education. I currently find myself in dire need of a new attendant and your son seems to fit the bill. So, what say you, farmer?"

Hapu glanced down at his son and shook his head in disappointment, before replying, "Forgive me sir, but I do not have two bars of gold. Would you consider accepting less?"

Again, the charioteer let out his hearty, loud laugh and said, "You've got it completely wrong, man! I am prepared to pay YOU two bars of gold, for depriving you of the lad's services. A boy of his size must be quite useful around your farm. Unless, that is, I am completely wrong about his abilities!"
Reaching into his pouch, Ay took out the small pieces of gold and offered them to Hapu. He walked over to the chariot and took them, almost reluctantly from the visitor's hand. Then, the charismatic stranger turned and said to Nakht, "Say goodbye to your family, boy. But please make it quick. Otherwise I'll be late for dinner."

While his father took the money from Ay, Nakht intoned a silent prayer of thanks to the god of fate. Then he swiftly hugged his family and hopped up onto the chariot. The youth felt like a King already, as his former neighbours watched his departure, with their chins trailing, open mouthed and almost on the ground.

Chapter Three

On the morning after the Hittites had been ambushed, Nakht rose with the sun. Djar, his second in command was already up and rousing the rest of the men. Nakht cleaned his hands and face in the sand. There was no time for any of them to bathe in the oasis' waters. After a sparse breakfast of bread and water, the horses were untethered and hitched up to the chariots. They had a long day's drive ahead of them to reach the fortified town of Gosa. From there it would be another seven days' ride to Avaris. This was an important town on a tributary in the northern delta, where they had left their Nile transport. It was at Avaris that the Theban Pharaoh Khamose had first defeated the conquering Hyksos. Then there would be another four days of sailing against the Nile's current, but with the prevailing wind, until they reached Thebes. Time was of the essence. Nakht was no longer worried about the possibility of pursuit by the Hittites. If there had been a trailing second party they would have discovered the bodies by now. But he was worried about Ay's wedding, which was due to take place within eleven days. Because Zannanza's severed hand was to be the bride's wedding gift, from her prospective husband, they had to make good time. If Ay's token of affection arrived late, there was every chance of the wedding being called off or postponed. And the grand Vizier did not like his plans to be disrupted by even one moment.

Of course none of the other soldiers, not even Djar, were aware of this. As far as they were concerned it was a routine military action against a detested northern enemy. Obviously they knew that Ay was involved. Nakht's very presence amongst them was sufficient to make the men aware of that. And they had all seen the cuneiform tablet, which he had showed to the Hittite prince. They could make of that what they would. But even the severing of the dead man's hand was nothing out of the ordinary. It was Egypt's traditional way of proving that an enemy had been killed. Besides, the men had served in the regiment long enough to know that Nakht's orders were never to be questioned. They might be explained, but only if the Commander felt it necessary to do so.

There were two men to each chariot and Nakht shared his with Djar. When all the men were ready, Djar boarded their chariot and gave the signal to move out. His Commander gestured silently towards the reigns and his deputy inclined his head, before taking them up. Then he pulled the leather straps back hard, released the pressure slightly and the twelve chariots set off for Gosa. Nakht grasped the side of the vehicle firmly and prepared himself for a long morning's ride. No longer being a chatty person, *he retreated back into the thoughts that had kept him sane the previous night...*

...After riding out of Bathar, on the back of Ay's chariot, the next few weeks of Nakht's young life had sped by in a blur. He had accompanied Ay on the remainder of his hunting trip around the delta. The soldier has introduced him to the rest of his party, which included a junior officer called Horemheb, as, "The young man who wants to see Amun's house. I gather that his father is solely responsible for its construction."

Whenever Ay related this story his audience would collapse in fits of laughter. Nakht knew they were laughing at him, but was unable to see the joke. After all, his father had taught him that the god lived in a specially built house upstream of Bathar. This anecdote was often related over dinner after a long day's sport. Although Nakht was not permitted to sit at the table, he was allowed to stand at Ay's side. One of his earliest duties was to ensure that his master's wine was constantly replenished. When his guests had finished dining Ay gave him permission to eat from what was left on the table. On several occasions, the dinner guests stayed behind to watch as the boy gorged himself on beef and wildfowl, the like of which he had never before tasted in his life. This was then washed down with a large draft of leftover red wine, which made him keep bumping into the room's furniture.

At night he slept on a mat at the foot of Ay's bed, wrapped in a light sheet. His master's bedroom was larger than the brick house that he had grown up in. Nakht could not understand how one person needed so much space just to sleep in. On their first night together, he had been given quite a fright. Just before Ay had climbed into bed, he had removed his entire head of hair and placed it on a side table. It was the first time that the boy had seen a wig made of human hair. Men and woman from his village wore wigs, although these were made out of fibres from crop wastage or papyrus stems. But every day contained something newer and better than he was used to in Bathar. Like the time that the hunting trip in the delta came to an end. It was a moment that he had been dreading, because at the back of his mind was the fear that he would be sent back to his village.

That night, before the guests assembled for dinner, Ay took Nakht to one side. He patiently explained that his royal duties meant that he must return to Thebes on the following day. And if Nakht wished to accompany him then certain things had to change. For a start he had to bathe regularly, as the people who lived in that city were not used to mixing with dirty people. Nakht also had to dress like a member of a very important household. The boy's face fell at the second condition. Other than his tiny cloth apron he had no garments and no means of purchasing any. Briefly, Nakht thought that he would have to return to Bathar and his father would have to refund the gold bars. That was until Ay reached into a trunk and pulled out a youth's linen kilt and a pair of leather sandals. With a smile on his face, he threw them one by one at the boy. Nakht caught the gifts and thought that he had already reached the afterlife. Now he could dress like a scribe, before he could even read or write a single word. But there was one final condition. Although he would always be able to eat his fill, when they were in Thebes, Nakht must not devour beef, pork or fowl like a wild animal. This, Ay assured him, was something else that the people of Thebes did not like to see. For his own part, the boy thought that the inhabitants of Thebes must be the most incredibly refined people in the whole of the known world. But as at least his new patron had not forbidden him from belching or farting, that was a small crumb of comfort to hang onto.

On the following morning they set out from Bubastis. This was the city of Bast, the cat headed god whose festivals were noted for their great revelry. Ay's hunting party was heading for Thebes in a large, river sailing boat. They had the benefit of the northerly wind behind them to send them on their way. Nakht was wearing his new kilt and sandals. As he came on board, the youth was full of exhilaration at the prospect of the trip. But he tried very hard not to show it. He had stayed awake all night listening to Ay snoring. It hadn't been the noise that had kept him awake, but his determination to think of ways that he could avoid showing up his master. The boy was painfully aware of his humble background and wanted to succeed in his new life. So on the boat, he refrained from jumping up and down and tried to behave like a young gentleman.

Both Ay and Horemheb noticed with some amusement this new, reserved side of the youth. The latter, a fairly seriously minded man, even allowed a rare smile to crease his lips. The journey up the Nile was like a pleasure cruise for the boy. His only regret was that they were not going to pass his village, so he couldn't wave to his parents. But the ship's crew found the journey harder going. The vessel was travelling south, against the flow of the river. When the wind dropped they had to take to the oars and stretch their backs.

On the second day, they passed Ghiza and Nakht saw the great pyramids for the first time. His father had been speaking the truth and such buildings did exist. As he stared with wide eyes at the western plateau, his new found reserve finally left him. Rushing up to Horemheb, who was standing on the deck he shouted, "Please, Lordship, tell me who do those houses belong to?"

The junior officer had also been staring at the ancient monuments. Initially, he was less than pleased to have had his thoughts interrupted. But realising that the boy needed to be educated he said, "They are the houses of the dead. Pharaohs who ruled Egypt over a thousand years ago, sleep peacefully inside them. Actually, you should know that they are called pyramids are not houses, in the normal sense of the word. They are the ancient Pharaohs' tombs of eternity."

Nakht thanked the man gracefully for his explanation and left him to return to his thoughts. He was not sure whether he entirely liked the tall young officer. This was because Horemheb always appeared to look at him in an unfriendly and mean manner. And when he spoke, he seemed to snap at him. The youth was pleased that Ay was his master rather than the young officer.

During the course of the voyage, Ay seemed quite pleased with the progress that his young retainer was making. In the evenings, he noted that although the youth was not eating sparingly, he was behaving with some decorum at the table. Nakht was also being discreet in his consumption of wine. After dinner, rather than pouring down his throat what was left of the high status drink, he sipped at it. Ay began to think that his protégée might adapt well to his new life in Thebes. But he made a mental note to talk seriously to the boy about his propensity for passing wind. It seemed to come from both ends, without provocation, after he had taken food and drink. The older man put this down to Nakht's upbringing and the fact that he was not used to such rich produce. Either way it had to stop. Horemheb's pained expression at mealtime was not only due to his stern outlook on life but in part down to Nakht's bodily emissions.

Nakht had only seen the pyramids on the Ghiza plateau in the distance, so he had no chance to see if they were taller than mountains. Maybe if he had, then the boy would have been better prepared for the splendour of Thebes. For somebody who had grown up in a village of fifty small houses he was totally unprepared for its size and magnificence. Of course, he had seen other cities from the boat on the journey up the Nile. But other than a brief stop, so that Ay and Horemheb could stretch their legs, he had had no chance to explore them. At the end of the voyage, his naivety showed through again. It was just after Ay had told him their destination was only a short distance away. Nakht positioned himself at the prow of the ship, anxious to get his first glimpse of Thebes. He was unaware that heading south on the Nile, they would approach the temples of Karnak before docking at Thebes. From his position in the prow, he saw the tall and brightly coloured buildings of Karnak. Feeling excited he shouted loudly, "My Lord Ay, I can see Thebes! Whose pyramids are those?"

Ay joined him on the prow and smiled before answering, "Boy, what you see is Karnak. It is a part of Thebes, but it is on the opposite side of the river to where we are going. And you are not looking at any pyramids. The pyramids of Ghiza are shaped like triangles. Those buildings ahead of us are temples and the first one belongs to Amun. When we first met, in your village, you called it Amun's house."

Horemheb, who had joined them at the front of the boat said to Ay, with more than a trace of exasperation in his voice, "You indulge the lad too much, Ay. He is only your junior servant, after all."

Nakht ignored the junior officer's disparaging words. But Ay didn't. He turned to face Horemheb. Then he sighed and answered, "Are we not all servants of one rank or another? What else do we all do but the serve the Pharaoh and our country? We are lucky enough to perform our duty in the army. But this youth and his ilk grow the very food that our nation eats. Is that not also a worthwhile form of service?"

The younger officer did not reply. He knew that when Ay had that tone in his voice, he would not listen to him reason. Nakht also continued to hold his tongue and slipped away to the rear of the vessel. The crew were paying out the ropes, in preparation for berthing the ship on the west bank of the river. He enjoyed helping them to do that job.

Once they were ashore, Ay and Horemheb went their separate ways. There was still an air of slight animosity between them, which could be detected in the manner that they made their farewells. Nakht carried his master's linen bags in Ay's wake, as he led the way through the noisy, bustling crowds. Nakht was amazed not only at the noise, but at the profusion of colours and smells. They were all completely new to him. Several beggars approached his master, but Ay thrust them forcefully to one side. They also had to push through a busy market place, which had grown up some distance from the front of the Pharaoh's mortuary temple. Although the Valley of the Kings was strictly off limits to the populace, the immediate west bank was not. When they had walked against the human tide for several minutes and finally distanced themselves from the crowd, Ay called the youth to his side and said, "Well lad, this is Thebes. For better or worse. But there are another couple of ground rules that you need to know. Firstly, you must stop belching and farting after eating. It will not go down very well here – take my word for that. Secondly, my wife Tiy runs the house and is not to be argued with. Whatever she says to you, just bite your tongue and bow your head. The Amun knows that I have done the same these past ten years. And thirdly, as a servant you must report to my butler Hor. If anything he's a lot worse than my wife, but unfortunately he is a great favourite of hers. Don't mind him though, just do as I do and just humour the man."

    Nakht had heard the words but couldn't begin to understand Ay's logic. How could such a strong and powerful Lord be bullied in his own home? But a little voice at the back of his mind told him that he would soon enough find out. Although first, he had to get over the immense size of Ay's property. As they arrived at the estate the boy's eyes started to pop out of his head. Nothing that he had seen, not even the captain's holiday home in the delta, had prepared him for this. It was bigger than the entire village of Bathar, once the grounds were included. Together they strolled through the gardens, the boy looking in amazement at the plants and water features. Finally, they reached the front entrance, a large door flanked by lotus bud columns. As soon as they were inside the hallway a man, who was slightly older than Ay appeared. Before he could speak Ay bowed down and whispered to Nakht,

"As I said, just bite your tongue, lad...this is where the fun begins!" Then he looked up at the man in the hallway and said, "Hor, how nice it is to see you here, to welcome me upon my return from the delta!"

The thin butler inclined his shoulders slightly, although not over respectfully. He even smiled in a pained way. But all the time his gaze was fixed on Nakht. With the civilities over he sniffed and said to Ay, "I'll take your bags from the beggar, sir. It was very kind of you to allow him to carry them here. With your permission, I'll give him a small token of payment and send him..."

"You'll do nothing of the sort," Ay interrupted, "Tell me Hor, when was the last time that you saw a beggar wearing a new linen kilt and leather sandals?"

The butler raised his eyes to the hall's tall ceiling and replied, "Very good, sir. Whatever you say. The lady Tiy waits your return in the sitting room. She is most anxious to see you. What shall I do with your...er...young man?"

"Nothing yet," was the terse response, "That is until I have introduced the latest member of our household to my wife."

Nakht watched as the butler forced another smile onto his angular face, before leading them through a long corridor. When they reached their destination, Hor preceded them into the sitting room and announced loudly,

"My lady, your husband and a...er...young man have arrived to see you."

Ay walked into the room first, indicating to Nakht that he should follow behind him. The youth's eyes

widened even further as he looked at the size of the room, its delicately painted walls and luxurious furnishings. But he was swiftly brought down to earth. The rather plump woman, who was reclining on a couch in the centre of the room, fixed her gaze on him and said acidly,
"Ay, please tell me, what exactly is that thing by your side. If you have brought another marsh urchin into our household, then I will not be in the slightest bit pleased!"

"But Tiy, darling, I have been looking for a new attendant since Gerah was sent to Kush. That was over a year ago!"

Ay's wife rose to her feet. This was not without a little difficulty because of her weight. She then paced around the room for a few moments, before shouting, "Sometimes Ay, you are totally beyond me. Now, just get him out of my sight, before I lose my temper with you completely!"

Her tone implied that she would brook no argument. Ay seemed to be in no mood to offer one. So he gestured for Nakht to leave the room swiftly. And that was the young man's introduction to a high status household in Thebes. After such a hostile welcome he was glad that he hadn't had a sudden attack of wind. That could have only made matters worse. He left the room in a hurry and left Ay to the not so tender mercies of his wife.

Chapter Four

Djar drove the chariot towards the Sinai desert until the sun reached its mid point in the sky. Then the soldiers stopped to eat and drink the last of their provisions from the outward journey. Nakht was not concerned about the fact that their supplies were now exhausted. Gosa was now much less than a half day's drive away and he was sure that they would reach their destination before the sun set. To encourage the men, he stood up and said, while they were finishing lunch, "We are making good progress. But as time is of the essence we must keep it up. Understood?" They all nodded in agreement, but with a slight amount of resentment present on their faces. Then, to their amazement Nakht uttered a rare second sentence, "I don't just mean for today, but for the whole of the next ten days. And that includes helping to row our transport against the current, if the north wind fails us. When we reach Thebes you can rest, you lazy bastards." Without waiting for a response, he boarded the chariot and waited for Djar to dismiss the men. When his second in command joined him, Nakht assumed the reigns, saying only, "It's my turn."

That meant it was Djar's turn to brace himself against the side of the chariot, as they set off on the afternoon's drive. Nakht was pleased to be steering the horses. He had to concentrate on following the barely existent trail, as best he could. By now, there were large rocks and rotted tree stumps to avoid, either of which could take a vehicle's wheel off. But at least the driving stopped his thoughts. For several months now, day or night, unless he was totally occupied his mind felt as if it were going to explode. He had consulted the regiment's doctor, but all he had told him to do was to relax. Try to take things easy and not get so upset. Although relaxation was impossible when the future of the two Kingdoms and Ay's ambitions were at stake. But suddenly, he felt a jab in his ribs from his second in command who yelled, above the noise of the chariot's wheels and horses, "I'm sorry, sir, but you nearly hit that last outcrop. Do you want me to drive ?"

Nakht shook his head and focused his attention on the horses and the road ahead. With a superhuman effort he managed to keep his mind clear, with only a few distractions, until the party reached its destination at Gosa.

There the soldiers were received well by the outlying garrison. They were glad to see a full complement return from what they had assumed to have been a dangerous mission. Nakht gave his permission for the men to be entertained in the soldiers' mess that night. Although this was on the strict understanding that his troops would be ready to depart when the sun rose. The garrison's Commander, a career soldier called Mehy, was honoured to have Nakht as his private guest. He was immediately escorted to the Commander's living quarters while Djar and the others billeted themselves in the barracks. The tall soldier was something of a living legend in the Pharaoh's armed forces and his influence with Ay was well known. Mehy was an intelligent and well presented officer, who appeared to be in charge of his command. He was a slim man, who was in his early thirties and did not seem to enjoy being away from the centre of power.

Over dinner Nakht made polite conversation, despite Mehy's probings, carefully guarding the true reason for their mission. At the same time he forced copious volumes of wine down his throat, in the hope that later in the night he would be able to sleep. Nakht knew that his host couldn't miss noticing the amount that he was consuming. But he didn't want him to see the sweats that the lack of alcohol brought on. This was something else that he had been living with for some time. But Mehy was the sole of discretion. Other than asking Nakht to try and end his exile in Gosa, he said very little when he realised that the taciturn soldier was going to give him no change. Finally, after assuring the Commander that he would press his claims for being recalled with Ay, Nakht was then allowed to go to his room.

    There he slept for three hours, until he awoke in his customary cold sweat. It was always the same, no matter how much he drank. Rising from the bed, Nakht walked over to a side wall and pulled up a chair. It was no use trying to get back to sleep. Once the effects of the red wine had worn off, then getting back to sleep was completely impossible. After sitting for a few minutes, he remembered that he was on the upper floor of the building. So there had to be an exit to the roof close by. He found it at the head of a small row of stairs, just outside his room. Grabbing a sheet from his bed, he climbed out into the open and lay down. Nakht looked up at the stars for a while and let the memories flood back into his mind. Once he couldn't sleep it was pointless to resist them. *In no time at all, he was back in Thebes...*

    ...A twelve year old boy staying in the house of Ay. Ostensibly, a servant or attendant to the captain, but a marsh urchin to everyone else in the household. It had been very hard for him at first, in the face of overt hostility from Tiy and the butler. But he consoled himself with the thought that he was on the way to a better life. Since leaving the village Nakht had not had to tend any crops, fish the river or harvest papyrus. From that time he had dressed like a high status youth, ate well and even learnt some table manners. Plus, his

father now had two gold bars to his name. That represented untold riches in their small village. In short, everybody had won. But Nakht did miss his family, especially when Tiy or the butler were rude and unfair towards him. There were no children for him to play with on Ay's estate. So he had to make his own amusements when his jobs were done.

It was not as if Ay had ignored the boy after they arrived in Thebes. But his interest in Nakht seemed to diminish. The youth was bright enough to realise that this was down to the pressures of attending the Pharaoh's household at the nearby palace of Malkata. Ay had to do this on a daily basis and often did not get back until late. But one day, as the captain was leaving for Amenhotep IV's court, he decided to take his chance. Unseen by Tiy or Hor, Nakht slipped out of the house and ran alongside his benefactor in the street. When Ay saw him he looked surprised and asked, "And what is troubling my young friend? Isn't my butler keeping you busy enough around the house?"

"Of course he is, sir. But please forgive me Lord, that was not our deal. When you bought me from my father, it was to learn to be a soldier. You also said that I could learn to read and write if I wanted to..." Nakht let his voice tail off and smiled at Ay innocently, any further words unnecessary.

The older man glanced down at him, as if he was making sure that Nakht appeared presentable. Then he looked behind himself at the house before saying, "Well then, I suppose that you'd better come with me to the palace. You can spend some time with the scribes, while I wait on the King and his grand Vizier. But I honestly do not know which of us will be the most bored!"

At the palace of Malkata, which Nakht noticed was at least four times the size of Ay's home, he was deposited with the Chief Scribe. The soldier had told him to keep both his tongue and wind still. But he had also told the Chief Scribe, in no uncertain terms, that the boy was to be taught how to read and write. Although the Chief Scribe was less than enthusiastic about this, he bowed to Ay's authority. Accordingly, Nakht was deposited with the most junior member of his office, who gave him a wax tablet and a stylus. The young scribe then started the task of teaching the youth his alphabet. While he formed and then rubbed out the hieroglyphs, Nakht snatched surreptitious glances at the Chief Scribe. He was a small man of some fifty years of age. Although he wore a long kilt and leather sandals, they were no better than the ones that Nakht was wearing. The boy realised what a fool he had been, to think that the chariot driving Ay had been this old man, when he had arrived in Bathar.

His education continued in this manner for the next two years. By the time he was fourteen Nakht could read and write as well as any scribe in the office. He could also draw up an official script on papyrus – without making any mistakes. Even the Chief Scribe had eventually warmed to him, realising that he was a fast and dedicated learner. The youth was then put to work on transcribing ancient texts from the King's library, which were in danger of rotting away. It was a task that he relished and accomplished quickly. Nakht had changed greatly in the intervening two years, both physically and mentally. He had continued to grow at a rapid pace, both upwards and across his shoulders. Most people took him to be between sixteen and eighteen years of age. His work in the scribe's office had started to hone his mind, as he had studied over a thousand years of Egypt's history and current affairs. When he walked to the palace with Ay, he was able to sensibly discuss the affairs of state that his master would have to deal with.

Nakht understood from Ay that Egypt was about to enter a transitional phase. Amenhotep III was no longer a young man. He had been the Pharaoh for more than thirty years. The army had been idle for most of this time due to the King's skill as a diplomat. People from far beyond the sea, that the Nile flowed into, came to visit him in the palace and seek his good will. This had guaranteed the country's security and increased its wealth through trade. Well, that was what Ay had told the youth and he had no reason to disbelieve him. But now that the King was in middle age it was time to make his son a co-regent. Amenhotep IV would share the throne with his father, until the latter died. Then he would become King in his own right. It struck Nakht as an equitable arrangement. Why should the older man not share his power? His son would benefit from the experience, so that when his father went to the afterlife, the heir would know what the job entailed. It all made good sense to him.

Although Nakht heard from his master that there were some problems in the double Kingdom of upper and lower Egypt. To his dismay, Ay had told him that the priesthood of Karnak were causing trouble. Like his father in Bathar, the young man worshipped Amun and at first refused to believe his master. But when Ay told him that the High Priest had caused a certain carving to be engraved in the white chapel at Karnak, Nakht's blood ran cold. The carving showed the High Priest actually equal to the Pharaoh in the sight of Amun! It seemed as if he was taking his official title, which was the first priest of Amun, far too seriously. Of course Amenhotep III had been very angry and his son more so. The younger man, who was also called Amenhotep, seemed to take the High Priest's slight very personally.

His father had summoned the most senior members of the priesthood to his court, in the temple of Luxor and set them straight in no uncertain terms. He was the King and it was his job alone to intercede with the gods as the first without equals. And for over thirty years he had done a good job of it. Egypt had been at peace with her neighbours and the land was more prosperous than it had ever been. Ay told Nakht that Amenhotep III had informed the priests that if such blasphemy ever occurred again, he would have no compunction in sending a detachment of his best guards to see them. For good measure the Pharaoh immediately ordered the white chapel to be torn down. Its rubble was to be used as fill, for a pylon that the King was in the process of constructing at Karnak.

    There was one other problem, far less serious than the attitude of the priesthood or the Pharaoh's age. It concerned a foreign territory in Nubia, which was under the rule of Egypt. From time to time, the people of Kush, which was a part of Nubia, rose up in small scale rebellions. News had recently reached Thebes of another such uprising. Nubia was an important territory for Egypt, as most of her gold was mined there. So both the Amenhoteps had decided that a policing expedition should be mounted to put down the rebels. The good news for Nakht was that Ay had been asked to lead it, in place of the two Kings. They had far more important matters of state to contend with. The even better news, was that his master had asked Nakht to share his chariot. The excited youth was going to escape from the scribe's office and become a soldier after all. There was only one cloud on his horizon. The surly Horemheb was to be the second in command to Ay. But Nakht was not too worried about that. An expedition to the south of the country was something for a young man to look forward to.

Chapter Five

    For the rest of that night in Gosa, Nakht lay on the roof and stared up at the heavens. In Egypt's ancient history, the stars had been very important to the earlier dynasties of Pharaohs. At the very start of his service to Ay, the work in the library at Malkata had taught him that the great pyramids at Ghiza had been aligned with the belt of Orion. But despite his studies, Nakht was still unable to see the stars' significance in the modern age or appreciate their importance to earlier generations. It was with some relief, that he eventually caught sight of the rising sun. Another night was finally over. From the ground below him he heard the sounds of soldiers leaving the barracks building. The noises were caused by his own men and the garrison's dawn patrol. He watched disinterestedly as Djar supervised the their own preparations and Gosa's dawn patrol moved off to relieve their comrades. After fresh horses had been hitched to the chariots, provisions were loaded up. They had six days of hard driving left before they reached Avaris. Gosa was the last town able to properly accommodate his force until then. The next six nights would be spent sleeping underneath the stars. It would be no great hardship, provided they could find water for the horses. That should not be a problem, as they had found it on the way there. But as most soldiers were aware, such supplies could easily dry up.

    Nakht raised himself from the roof and went down to the Commander's guest room. There he groomed himself, before going down to the ground floor. Mehy was waiting for him at the foot of the stairs and said, "I hope that you slept well. The gods will protect you on your journey to Averis, my friend. And please don't forget your little promise from last night, to talk to Lord

Ay. I'll make it worth your while when I am recalled to Thebes – you have my word on that."

Nakht thought to himself that Mehy didn't know how lucky he was. From his own experience it seemed better for both body and soul if Ay was completely unaware of your existence. All the same he replied, "I'll speak to the grand Vizier as soon as I can. But, now, we must be away. Thank you for looking after us."

"It was no trouble at all. And by the way, I had my slave slip a fairly, decent sized skin of red wine into your provisions. Just in case you fancy a drink when the sun goes down, on your way back. It should last you…"

With the pleasantries concluded, he was able to rejoin his men in the courtyard. Djar had the men stood by their chariots ready to climb aboard. Nakht nodded his head at him, a gesture of appreciation for the subordinate's good work. Then he said loudly, "Six more days of hard work in the sun, men. After that we'll be across the Sinai desert and in Avaris. So let's move."

Djar took the reigns for the morning's drive and they soon left the fortified town behind them. At least the sun was on their backs, as they were heading west. It made the arduous job of steering an unwieldy vehicle slightly easier. *The first time that Nakht had steered a chariot was in preparation for Ay's punitive expedition to lower Nubia…*

…After he had gleefully accepted the captain's invitation to share his chariot, Nakht was excused from the Chief Scribe's office. Ay assigned the youth to the barracks for two months, for basic military training, while he assembled the expedition. Although he was really too young to train as a soldier, especially with a crack regiment, his size and his patron's power worked in his favour. There were many things that Nakht learned in those two months, other than how to steer a chariot. The youth was taught how to use a sword,

throw a spear and fire a bow. He also learnt about his own unusual strength. It was the custom in the King's bodyguard for the soldiers to practice unarmed combat. Some of the older men, who knew that Ay was behind Nakht's advancement, had taken it upon themselves to teach him a lesson. These soldiers decided amongst themselves that the ideal classroom would be the training ground where they rehearsed their wrestling and throws

The ring leader of the little group was called Pteti, a veteran non-commissioned officer. He was not taken at all by Nakht and regarded him as a jumped up country boy, who had a powerful sponsor. Not all of his comrades shared this view. Most thought that he had done well with the sword and the spear, for a person of his age. They had also been impressed with the way that he handled a bow. More than a few were from a similar background. Men who had grown up in small farming villages, who remembered how hard it had been to escape. So they didn't begrudge him his stroke of luck in finding a wealthy patron. But on the other hand they were not prepared to cross Pteti, a man known for harbouring grudges. So when the soldiers arrived at the training ground and Pteti paired himself off with Nakht their were no dissenting voices. Although all the other men did stop their own practice and prepared to watch the contest.

Nakht had no idea of what lay in store for him. If anything he was flattered that the non commissioned officer had chosen him as a partner. He bowed his head, in respect and said, "What do you want me to do, sir?"

"Just pretend that I am your enemy and run at me as hard as you like. Imagine that you have a dagger in you right hand and you are going to plunge it into my chest..." Pteti backed away from him and assumed a crouching position. Nakht also moved backwards and then began his charge. The older man held his ground, until the youth was almost upon him. Then he rose to his full height and stepped to one side. Nakht saw the movement but his momentum carried him on. Straight onto the outstretched arm, which Pteti had locked and swung firmly, at neck height. It connected with Nakht's throat, jarring his head backwards at an alarming angle. Several of the other soldiers winced, as the young man crumpled on to the dusty ground. Pteti barely stifled a smile and shrugged his shoulders at the onlookers. Then he said, "Take the boy back to the barracks. He'll be out for the rest of the day."

As he had already turned his back on Nakht, he was not aware that his young adversary had risen to his feet. But the expression on the faces of the men in front of Pteti indicated that his words may have been premature. He turned around to see the youth dusting himself down. Nakht glanced up at him and said as he caught his breath, "That..that...was a very good hit, sir. I did see it coming but couldn't stop myself. Can we try it again?"

Pteti was left with no choice but to agree. By rights the blow from his trailing arm should have knocked the boy's head off. The two then backed away from each other again and Nakht resumed his charge. This time the non-commissioned officer moved away to the other side and kicked the youth's legs from underneath him. Nakht crashed down face first. His body made a loud thumping sound as he crashed to the ground. By now, after seeing him take two hard hits, most of the other soldiers were willing Nakht to get up. He didn't disappoint them. Once again, he swiftly rose to his feet, wiped off the dust and said breathlessly, "Perhaps...it..will be third time lucky, sir?"

Pteti was wondering what he had to do to lay this boy out. It was beyond belief that the youth could shrug off such physical punishment. But he still had a few moves left, so he indicated for the boy to return to his starting place. Once more Nakht charged forwards, waving his imaginary dagger at Pteti. The older soldier held his crouch. Then he moved forwards at the last moment and threw a right upper cut which landed squarely on Nakht's jaw. The resulting cracking sound was heard throughout the barracks. For the third time, the youth fell down, amidst groans from those watching. And yet again he rose to his feet, but not quite as quickly as the other two times. Perhaps, he was also more than a little shaky on his feet. But Nakht still managed to force a smile onto his face and managed to say, as he rubbed his chin, "Again, sir? I could certainly manage another go. If that's all right with you?"

The men applauded his spirit by clapping their hands loudly. Pteti sensed that his little ruse was now working against him. Rather brusquely, he sent the youth away to practice with somebody else. But Nakht was the only winner that day, even though he had not even laid a hand on the non commissioned officer. His new comrades were more than impressed with the youth's courage and durability. Before the day was out, rumours started circulating in the barracks about the raw strength of the marsh boy from the delta. It was the start of what came to be known in the Pharaoh's army as the legend of Nakht. And Pteti was quite definitely the loser. He acquired the long and unflattering nickname of, "He who could not lay out an unarmed fourteen year old boy in three attempts". For ease of use in conversation, the men soon shortened this to "That useless arse hole". All the same, for several days Nakht's body hurt like he had never known it to hurt. Especially his chin, which felt as if a chariot had driven over it. But he just thought it to be a good idea to let nobody know about the pain that he was suffering from. If his comrades wanted to think of him as a strong marsh boy, then Nakht was not going to disabuse them.

    Of course news about this episode was quickly relayed to Ay. He was very pleased with the showing that Nakht had made. It confirmed his belief that the boy had something very special about him. He had sensed an unfathomable quality in Nakht during his unscheduled stop in Bathar. That was the main reason why he had paid the boy's father two golden bars for him. He now had to work out just how best to bring Nakht on, and then how to put the finished article to good use. The captain made a mental note to cast an incantation spell to Bast, the beautiful cat-goddess. Her dual nature of good and evil appealed to him greatly. Ay even decided to make the spell that evening, while the day's events were fresh in the cat goddess's memory. He often sought Bast's guidance on matters of this sort. Her intuition usually turned out to be both as accurate and invaluable, as his very own. She always confirmed the proof and validity of his perceptions.

Chapter Six

The morning's chariot ride out of Gosa passed without any undue incidents. Nakht snapped out of his thoughts, just before they stopped for at the borehole for a break. Djar had led them at a fast, but not a reckless pace, through the desert. They had covered distance without putting too much strain on the horses. Not even Ay could ask for any more, Nakht muttered to himself while he was dismounting. He watched as his second command organised the watering of the horses. Now that the ambush was successfully concluded the horses were actually of more importance than his men. The party needed to cross the desert quickly to finish their mission. But that depended on the horses remaining in good shape. To a certain extent the men were now dispensable, although they still had a function to fulfil. Rebel nomadic tribesmen were known to frequent their planned route. If the party were attacked, then the force would need all the available weapons at its disposal to defeat them.

Once the horses had been tended to, the soldiers sat down and took a short break. Like Nakht, the men ate sparingly. Nobody had a great appetite for food, due to the extreme heat of the sun. The conversation was also quite stilted, as aching limbs were rested and energy conserved. Everyone was looking forward to reaching Avaris and the Nile, even if it meant swimming home. That would be far more preferable to the extreme dryness of the desert sands - Nile crocodiles and the odd hippopotamus not withstanding. After a while, Nakht decided that they had rested the horses sufficiently. He rose to his feet and said, "My bottom has had enough of this hot sand, even if yours have not. Let's be on our way."

Djar rose and followed him to their chariot. The rest of the men hauled themselves up and climbed into their vehicles. They all knew that Nakht was right. The horses were rested and sitting on the sand would not get them to Avaris any faster. Taking the lead, Nakht resumed the pace that Djar had set earlier. For two hours all went well, as they made good progress. But then the accident happened. One of the chariots veered out of control, ploughed into a sand bank and overturned. It could only be because the driver had lost concentration or fallen asleep. Nakht had to halt the party and assess the damage. Even before the vehicle was righted, it was obvious that the damage to the undercarriage was substantial. Making a quick decision he said, "You two men will have to return to Gosa. There is no possibility that your chariot can be repaired in this desert. Take your horses and supplies. And next time concentrate when you are driving the Pharaoh's property."

The two men bowed their heads in shame at his admonishment. Nakht also felt quite guilty himself, after nearly overturning his chariot the previous day. But with their food and water the two should safely make it to Gosa on foot. Unfortunately, there was no way that they could be squeezed onto the remaining vehicles. There was still a long journey ahead and the extra weight would tire the horses. As the two soldiers prepared themselves to follow his instructions, the rest of the party pulled away and resumed their journey.

It was almost dark when they reached the next borehole and their resting place for the night. Even Nakht ate a more substantial meal than usual, realising that he would need to build up his body's reserves for the following day. However, he did take the skin of red wine from his chariot before retiring for the night. After several hearty swigs he started to relax. Then before he could stop himself, *Nakht was stood in front of Amun's temple at Karnak, two paces behind Ay and Horemheb...*

...His crash course in military training had finished. Although the youth readily acknowledged that he had to learn a lot more before he could call himself a soldier. Ay's preparations for the expedition to Nubia were also finalised. The majority of his force had been shipped south on the previous day. All that remained of it in Thebes, was the Commander's transport. It was waiting in the harbour, for the senior officers to follow the rest of their men. But before embarking the two commanding officers wanted to make offerings to Amun. After they had crossed the river, Nakht stood in awe, in front of Amenhotep III's massive pylon. This led through the impressive transverse hall and into the middle temple's obelisk courtyard. Behind him was a barely prepared building site, where the King had planned to construct something called a hypostyle hall, which Ay explained would have a roof supported by columns. Although this work had been halted following his disagreements with the priesthood.

Inwardly, Nakht still winced, when he thought about how he used to call the building "Amun's house". By now he had realised that the complex at Karnak actually comprised of three separate religious buildings. The northern temple was dedicated to Menthu, the Lord of Thebes and a local deity. The southern temple was dedicated to Mut, mother goddess of the New Kingdom and the wife of Amun. And the middle temple belonged to Amun, the powerful King of all gods. They were the three gods that had protected Thebes from ancient times and saved Egypt from the Hyksos. Although recently Amun had risen greatly in popularity. His following had eclipsed the worship of other deities, not just in Thebes but throughout the whole of Egypt. Amun was now also known as Amun-Re. His hidden powers were combined with the life giving force of Re, the sun god. So there was no deity able to match him for power or popularity.

In front of the small party, Ay's slaves carried offerings for Amun. There was gold, the carcass of a bull and a large amphora of wine. Such munificent sacrifices were being made to ensure the success of their mission, which was to subdue the recalcitrant inhabitants of Kush. As they walked through the main entrance and passed through the transverse hall, into the obelisk courtyard, they were approached by the temple's Chief or High Priest. He was a thin, elderly man who had what Nakht could only describe as piercing eyes, which seemed to stare deep into a person's mind. Like his important important visitors, the High Priest was well aware of the political significance of the expedition to Nubia. So although he had already crossed swords with Ay several times, the Chief Priest had to be seen to want the mission to succeed. Hence, he presented himself in the courtyard wearing his ceremonial leopard skin cloak. In front of one of Tuthmosis III's obelisks he accepted the offerings. This was done on behalf of Amun, with some grace and dignity. As his acolytes carried the offerings into the temple, Ay thanked the priest for his intercession and departed. Behind him the temple's chantresses and musicians struck up a hymn in praise of Amun. The obelisk courtyard was as far as men who were not members of the priesthood were allowed to venture. Common people were not even allowed that far. They had to content themselves with standing on Amenhotep III's building site, to gaze upon his impressive pylon.

It was certainly further into the temple complex than Nakht had ever been allowed before. He could barely take his eyes off the sheer majesty and size of the tall and brightly painted obelisks. The youth could hardly believe that they had been carved from the granite quarries in one single piece. And then shipped down the Nile, all the way from Aswan. Ay had told him that Amenhotep III had funded the construction of the pylon and various other improvements to the middle temple. The massive obelisks in the courtyard pre-dated his reign by some years. But the King had also built a new temple, in Luxor, to show the Karnak priesthood that he meant business in his dealings with them. This had been dedicated to Ma'at, the daughter of the sun god Re. Amenhotep III had also funded the construction of several other temples, at Kawa, Hebenu and Hermopolis and many other places. It was his clever way of showing the priesthood of Karnak that it did not have a monopoly upon religion.

As Nakht followed the two officers on their way to the harbour, Ay said to Horemheb, "At least the priesthood will be eating and drinking well tonight. Not to mention lining their deep pockets with yet a few more of our hard earned gold bars."

Horemheb grinned but did not reply. Nakht was puzzled at his master's words, not yet having realised what happened to offerings when they were removed from the temple's courtyard. He was taken aback even more when Ay continued, "Let the old hypocrite stuff his gut and fill his pockets while he can. I tell you Horemheb, the co-regent has had enough of the priesthood. Mark my words well, when he assumes the throne there will be a time of reckoning for those sanctimonious parasites!"

The second in command looked very uneasy at these words and gestured as if to say keep your voice down, there are too many people around.

During their journey up the Nile, Nakht heard several more disconcerting conversations, while he stood at Ay's shoulder, in company with Horemheb. Whenever the two older men were talking, he glanced down at the deck, pretending not to listen. Although he knew that the Commander was aware that he was taking in every word. Their most alarming discussion concerned the health of the Pharaoh, Amenhotep III. Nakht knew that he was not a young man, hence the reason for making his son the co-regent. But he was not aware of the serious nature of the man's illness. It seemed that every tooth in the King's head had rotted or was rotting away. Although their society had remedies or magic for almost any ailment, dentistry was the branch of medicine that was beyond them. Ay informed Horemheb that the King was in absolute and total agony every minute of the day. As a result, his family were giving him constant doses of red wine to dull the pain. The consequences were that he was always drunk and unable to grasp any issue, other than when his next cup of wine was due. The co-regent, now known as Amenhotep IV, was effectively the sole Pharaoh.

But Ay also had worrying news about him. Out of devotion to his father and the suffering that the great ruler was enduring, an amazing decision had been reached. Amenhotep IV had decided that his father should be worshipped as a living god. And not just any living god, but one superior to Amun-Re. The son had decided that the old man was the incarnation of the Aten. This was an obscure form of the sun god Re, represented only by the solar disc. Re without a body in fact. According to Ay, all of this would become known to the public at large after the successful completion of their expedition. He went onto relate that this was going to be the first step that the new King would take against the Karnak priesthood. But there would be more to follow. Amenhotep IV had no intention of ruling in the shadow of the Theban priests. They had already gone too far, by carving their own images in the white chapel, in place of the Pharaoh. Like Nakht, Horemheb listened in silence without making comment. But unlike the youth, he recognised the extremely serious implications of the young Pharaoh's proposals.

But before any of this could be put into effect, Amenhotep IV needed a victory over the Nubians to sway public opinion in his favour. The latest dispute with their southern neighbours centred around a non existent threat to the colonial gold mines. Because of political expediency it had been exaggerated out of all proportion. The facts were simple and straightforward. There had been a minor show of disobedience against Merymose, the Egyptian viceroy of Kush. The co-regent had seized upon this and portrayed it as a danger to Egypt's wealth and security. So Ay and Horemheb were sent south, with a force of a thousand men to face less than five hundred rebels. Victory was already assured. And plans were under way in the court, to announce the action to be as important as Amose's defeat of the Hyksos. Although the ensuing battle turned out to be little more than a policing action, meeting with slight resistance, it was significant to Nakht. Because it was near the Nubian city of Kerma that he killed his first man, some months before his fifteenth birthday.

The punitive expedition continued its journey up the Nile until they reached the third cataract. At this point they disembarked and marched south towards Kerma and Amenhotep III's fortress at Khaemmaat. The city of Kerma had been the independent capital of the Kingdom of Kush, before the Egyptians had brought Nubia under their control. In the surrounding area there were still pockets of resistance to Egyptian rule. But in the 130 years since Tuthmosis III's emphatic victory, most Nubians had settled down to life under Egypt. Many of their highest families had been assimilated into positions of authority within the colonial administration.

Although out in the hinterlands, dissent remained but resistance was normally passive. This particular dispute had been caused by a local tribe's refusal to accept Merymose's levy on their menfolk. Labour was needed to work the gold mines and slaves were in short supply. This was one of the consequences of so many years of peace. Two of Merymose's officials had been killed in the settlement. The viceroy had decided that this was an appropriate moment to remind the Nubians of Egypt's military might. And Amenhotep IV and his court had seized on the opportunity.

After bivouacking overnight at Khaemmaat, Ay marched his force into the hinterland, towards a tiny village. Although the villagers were outnumbered, by two to one, they had to stand and fight. They had killed two of the viceroy's men and flight would be futile. Ay would only hunt them down like wild dogs and then slaughter them individually. It was far better to to fight and die like men. So the two forces met on a plain and the one sided battle was over in less than an hour. Neither Ay or Nakht took any direct part in the combat. The Commander remained in his chariot, at the rear of his troops on slightly raised ground. From there he directed the drawing up of his lines of attack and issued the command for the battle to begin. First, the archers unleashed a murderous hail of arrows. This was followed by a chariot charge, flanked by the infantry. The chariots smashed into the enemy's ranks and the infantry swarmed into the gaps. Before long it was all over - the rebels did not have the numbers or the weaponry to offer prolonged resistance. Over half their number were killed outright, with the rest either wounded or taken as slaves. The Egyptians lost ten men and suffered a similar number of wounded.

After the fighting was ended, Ay toured the battlefield surveying his troops' handiwork. Nakht had been a little disappointed with the action. He had imagined Ay hurling his chariot into the middle of the fight and smiting the Nubians with mighty blows. But he realised that somebody had to direct the battle and that someone was the Commander, Ay. Horemheb had been more fortunate. Ay had given him the honour of leading the chariot charge. When he returned from the battle, he brought with him five severed hands, which he presented to the Commander. The Commander congratulated him on his bravery and resumed his tour of the devastation. At his side, Nakht sensed that the older man was searching for something specific, as he steered the chariot amongst the corpses. Finally Ay seemed to find what he had been searching for. It turned out to be a badly wounded Nubian, that the Egyptian soldiers had missed. Ay had decided that it was time for Nakht to face the test that the cat goddess Bast had recently suggested to him.

Nakht could see that the man was still alive, because he was breathing. But he was totally unprepared for what happened next. The Commander drew his sword and offered it to Nakht saying, "Take this and send him to the underworld. Then bring me his right hand!"

The youth swallowed and took the weapon. His hand was shaking slightly, as were his legs, when he dismounted from the chariot. Ay watched with interest as he walked over to the prone Nubian. The man was lying on his back and had an arrow sticking out of his side. Unable to move, the injured soldier's eyes widened with fear, as Nakht stood over him and drew back the sword. He hesitated for a moment, as he realised that he was about to kill another human being. But then, after remembering his lessons from the barracks, the youth brought the sword downwards. He plunged the weapon into the Nubian's stomach and sliced upwards towards the chest. There was a loud whooshing sound, as the man breathed his last and the air left his lungs. Nakht then casually severed the hand, picked it up and after walking back to the chariot, respectfully presented it to Ay.

The Commander was pleased. Apart from an understandable initial show of nerves, Nakht had carried out his orders to the letter. Ay was now sure that the young man did have exactly what he was looking for. If he could butcher a man in cold blood, at such a young age, then the possibilities were endless. Of course, Nakht was completely unaware of his patron's thoughts. But for the second time in the day he felt cheated. He had always expected to make his first kill in the heat of a battle, rather than its aftermath.

Chapter Seven

Nakht pushed the men and beasts hard, on the final leg of their journey to Avaris. The intervening five days had passed without any incident, other than the tedium of driving through the desert. Even his memories from Thebes had given him a rest, during that part of the journey. He was no longer worried about the horses, as he knew that they were now less than a day's drive from the delta town. But he was worried about Ay's impatience. The soldier knew that the old man would be fretting and expecting his arrival long before it was physically possible. So after a sparse breakfast, he had slung the almost empty skin of wine into the chariot and told Djar to set a fast pace. The men had followed his lead and the party reached the bore hole before the sun reached its high point. They rested just long enough to let the horses catch their breath and then resumed their journey. As usual Nakht had driven the chariot in the afternoon. His aggressive pace paid off, because they reached their destination with two hours of daylight still remaining. From the day that the mission had disembarked and started its journey to the Syrian border, the ship had been placed on ten minutes notice for departure. So once the chariots had been placed in the care of harbour officials, Nakht and his men boarded the ship. The sailors released the vessel's securing ropes and they began the journey upstream to Thebes.

Their ship was a vessel of the royal Egyptian navy, commanded by Habt, an Admiral who took his orders directly from the grand Vizier. It had a short, squat sail and space for fifteen oarsmen on each bow, when the prevailing north wind failed. The oars were also needed for a journey downstream, which was entirely against the wind. Such boats could and did sail, or row up and down the Nile, as far south as Punt. Although the Admiral knew next to nothing about the purpose of Nakht's mission, Ay had made him aware that it was of the utmost importance. So from the moment the boat had been re provisioned, he had kept his crew on standby. Making use of the available wind and remaining daylight he personally supervised the navigation of the vessel. Nakht, on the other hand retired to his berth accompanied by a large jug of beer. The thirst of the desert needed to be washed from his throat. He could wash away the dirt from his body in the morning.

    As soon as the twilight fell, the Admiral had his men lower the sail and moor the vessel. It was far too dangerous to proceed any further. Constantly shifting sand banks, collisions with moored vessels and other hazards awaited those foolhardy enough to proceed in darkness. And Ay had no use for fools, whatever their rank. When the vessel was secure he had his men prepare a meal for everyone. It was by no means a feast, but after their rations in the desert, the soldiers found it substantial. Even Nakht ate a good plate of food, supplemented by the dregs of his wine from Gosa. After the meal, out of earshot of the others, Habt tried to pump him for information by asking,

"I take it that you were successful in your endeavours? Please tell me that Lord Ay will not be angry upon our arrival in Thebes..."

    "Lord Ay will be angry," Nakht interrupted, "But through no fault of the mission or yourself. He will be angry because we are not with him already! Now, do you have any more wine? My personal supply is finished."

    The Admiral realised that was as much information as he would get from the tall army captain. So he excused himself and detailed a subordinate to bring

Nakht some more wine. It was obvious to him that the soldier's Commander was going to be as irritating on the return journey, as he had been on the outward leg. While his wine was being brought, Nakht had a quick word with Djar. He told the second in command to ensure that the men went to their rest early. If the wind failed them on the following day, there would be more than enough rowing to share around soldiers and sailors alike. *Then after a few more cups of wine, Nakht retired to his hammock...*

...Where he was still travelling the Nile, but heading North towards Thebes, with Ay and Horemheb many years earlier. They were returning from Kush after the victorious campaign against the rebels. Ay was beside himself with joy, seeing a future filled with preferment and promotion. He had given Amenhotep IV the victory that the King desired. The Pharaoh now had his pretext for tackling the Karnak priesthood. And what better man to have beside him than his successful military Commander? Horemheb was also quite pleased with the outcome of the battle. His personal tally of five warriors killed, by his trusty heavy axe, had been the highest of any man. It guaranteed him the honour of receiving the King's Gold. This was awarded by the Pharaoh for acts of extreme valour and would do his career no harm. But for once it was Nakht who was the most subdued of the three. He knew that the hand that he had presented to Ay was a hollow trophy. The Nubian had been unable to even move. There was no honour in the act. If anything, it had been a mercy killing of a suffering, mortally wounded man. The youth had realised that the man was in great pain and in his final death throes, as he had stood over him.

Although those who listened to Ay heard a totally different story. His version told of how a victorious Commander had been surveying the battle field in his chariot, when a Nubian warrior had leapt up at him. The man had obviously been playing dead and hiding under the bodies of his comrades. His attack had startled the horses, which Ay had struggled to control. Meanwhile, Nakht had grabbed his straight sword and jumped off the vehicle. Dodging the Nubian's spear, with one blow the youth had sliced the warrior's stomach open, all the way up to his chest. Ay told everyone that his attendant, a marsh boy of less than fifteen years, had saved his life. Of course, everybody who heard this version of events was more than impressed. In time. it became the second strand of his legend, but not one that Nakht took any pride in. Nakht also knew that Horemheb was not fooled by Ay's words in the slightest. He could tell that from the way in which the thin officer looked at him whenever the story was related. But how could Nakht dare to contradict Ay by telling the truth, which only the two of them knew? He could not and did not. All the same, he bore Horemheb's reproachful gaze with a resentful feeling of marked injustice.

Upon their return to Thebes, Ay and Horemheb were accorded a heroes' welcome. Amenhotep IV's propaganda machine had worked overtime, during their absence. People of all ranks clamoured at the docks to get a glimpse of the warriors who had saved Egypt. A day of celebrations was ordered for the safe return of the army and the restoration of order. All of this reflected well on the co-regent, in his subjects' eyes. Firstly, he had chosen wisely in assembling the force, especially in his choice of commanders. Secondly, he had seen a threat to the nation and moved both swiftly and decisively to crush it. Finally, and most importantly, his crucial intercession with the gods had ensured the mission's success. They had looked kindly on Egypt because of Amenhotep IV's tireless endeavours to placate them. Most people in Thebes were now aware of his father's infirmity. The older man was no longer seen in public. Although few were aware of the true nature of his illness, it was generally held to be serious. So as far as the populace was concerned, the success of the mission to Kush could be attributed to only one person – Amenhotep IV.

On the day of celebrations Ay woke Nakht early. He was surprised to be roused by his master and wondered what was going on. Before he could rub the sleep out of his eyes, Ay enlightened him by saying excitedly, "I've sent Hor to bring you a new kilt and sandals. Now get up and bathe, there's no time to lose. I've just received an urgent message. We are going to the palace for an audience with the Pharaoh. He wants to reward his heroes from Nubia, before the day of celebrations starts!"

Nakht jumped out of the bed feeling very excited himself at this news. But then his stomach dropped and he asked, "Am I to be rewarded, Lord Ay?"

"Most definitely! You are to receive the King's Gold of Honour, for saving my life. You, barely more than a boy, will be honoured by Amenhotep!"

"Alongside Horemheb?"

"Of course and some of the others from the army...what's wrong Nakht? Come on lad, you can tell me."

Ay could see the youth's pained expression as Nakht replied sheepishly,
"Horemheb knows that I didn't save your life. I can tell from the way that he looks at me..."

"Nonsense," Ay interjected, "He doesn't know that and even if he did I wouldn't care a fig. Horemheb is a hypocrite and a liar. There's no way that he could have killed five men himself. I didn't see enough Nubians to go round. in the first place, for one man to have slaughtered five of them. So stop feeling sorry for yourself and go and bathe yourself! I've already told you that there's no time to lose."

Confused, but feeling slightly better Nakht picked up his towel. Ay walked towards the door. But before leaving the room, the older man turned and said, "Nakht, I want you to remember one thing. If people believe a story then it happened. Do not let mere facts spoil something that runs in our favour. That way we will go far together. Understood, boy?"

The tone in Ay's voice was firm and laden with authority. Nakht took in his words and replied, "I think so...no, no, I do understand you, master."

It was Nakht's first visit to the palace of Malkata since he had finished working in the Chief Scribe's office. Along with Horemheb and several other soldiers, Ay and Nakht were kept waiting outside the King's throne room for a while. But for the first time since the battle, the youth was able to meet Horemheb's gaze without looking away. Eventually an official emerged from the throne room and announced, "The Pharaoh is ready to see you. Please proceed."

As the expedition's commanding officer Ay led the way. This meant that Nakht had to follow at his shoulder, being his personal attendant. So Horemheb and the other soldiers were forced to follow him into the throne room. Nakht had never been this far into the palace. He knew of its splendour but was unprepared for the sights that awaited him. Although on this occasion it was not the architecture that he was anticipating. It was the King and Queen. He had seen the Pharaoh at events such as the festival of Opet, but it had always been from a distance. Now he was about to come face to face with Egypt's ruler. The living god, who wore the dual crown of the two Kingdoms and the King's great wife – the glamorous and beautiful Nefertiti.

Like all the rooms in the palace, the throne room was brightly decorated and imposing in size and architecture. At the opposite end of the room to the entrance were two raised gold thrones. On one sat Amenhotep IV and on the other, sat the King's great wife Nefertiti. Standing at the King's shoulder was Ramose, his Vizier and the Governor of Thebes. Alongside him was another dignitary known as the fan bearer to the King's right side. Nakht found this title confusing, because the man was doing no fanning. Later Ay explained to him that it was an honorary role, denoting the official's rank and status. As they approached the royal couple, Nakht followed Ay and Horemheb's lead and prostrated himself on the floor. Feeling totally overawed, he kept his eyes closed. The Pharaoh waited briefly before smiling and saying, in a voice that has a strange lisp, "My heroes may now rise and come closer to the throne. You have my permission to stand."

The youth waited until Ay struggled back to his feet, before rising himself. Then almost hiding behind the back of his master, he followed him across the room towards the two thrones. When the party had closed to a respectful distance they halted and bowed their heads. Out of the corner of his eye, Nakht caught the Pharaoh smiling at his wife. Then the King turned away from her and stroked his lip with his right forefinger, several times before stating, "You may raise your heads and gaze upon me. Because of your great achievements in Kush, I am minded to allow all of you to see your ruler and his Queen!"

As Nakht raised his head he didn't know who to look at first. Amenhotep was the Pharaoh, but as a heterosexual, young male his eyes were irresistibly dragged in the direction of the Queen. Without a shadow of a doubt, she was incredibly beautiful. Her very name translated as "the beautiful one has arrived". In all of his life Nakht had never seen such a poised and elegant woman. Her facial features were greatly enhanced by the gold and turquoise necklace that she was wearing around her finely sculpted neck. But the jewellery only added to her perfection rather than contributing towards it. Despite his young age, he doubted that he ever would ever see such an attractive woman again. Incredibly, this divine creature was also Ay's daughter. His patron was extremely well connected, being a half brother of the Pharaoh's mother Queen Tiy. Nakht had originally found all of this to be very difficult to understand. But eventually he had realised that Amenhotep III's Queen Tiy was a different person and not related to the Tiy who was Ay's wife. And as confusing as it was, the young man had to accept that he had just seen Ay prostrate himself before his own son-in-law and daughter.

Nefertiti was undoubtedly the epitome of everything that was good and glamorous about Egyptian womanhood. But regrettably, the same case could not be made for her consort, in respect of Egyptian manhood. Putting it mildly, the Pharaoh had a very odd appearance. His face was elongated, as were his hands and fingers. The man's upper torso curved towards his hips in the manner of a woman's waist. And to top it all his stomach bulged out, as if he was at least four months with child. Knowing that it was rude to stare, especially at a living god, Nakht averted his gaze to back of Ay's head. The Commander was wearing his best wig and most expensive make up for this audience. But before Nakht could consider Ay's appearance any further, the Pharaoh raised his hand and said, "That is sufficient. You have now gazed upon me as much as I shall permit in a single audience! Ramose, let me make the presentations so that we can start the celebrations. They are long overdue."

The Vizier handed a scroll to the King. Ay was the first to be called forward. Amenhotep thanked him for quelling the rebellion and told him, "By way of reward, we have decided to raise your position in the royal household. Henceforth, you are to be the master of the King's horses. You may depart. When the festivities are over, you will take up your new position."

Ay backed away from the royal presence, bowing profusely. The other men, starting with Horemheb were called forward and received the King's Gold of Honour. Each award was handed out by the Vizier. Finally it was Nakht's turn. As he approached the throne, the Pharaoh looked across at his Queen and said, in an odd lisping voice, "Do you believe that this boy is not yet fifteen? He looks every bit eighteen years of age."

Nefertiti returned her husband's grin replying,"I am told that he is a marsh boy and of good farming stock. They are big and strong subjects from a young age. And very loyal."

Amenhotep nodded at her words, as Nakht shivered at the thought of the beautiful Nefertiti having prior knowledge of his existence. Meanwhile, the Pharaoh looked him up and down for a moment before saying, in somewhat over pitched tones, "Let nobody in Egypt say that progress is barred to any of my people. Even the humblest subject is entitled to the King's Gold if his actions merit it. I thank you for saving the life of my servant Ay. Here - take this boy and go and enjoy the day's celebrations."

Nakht muttered his embarrassed thanks and retreated to join the rest of his group.

Outside the palace, before they joined the festivities, Ay had some good news to tell him. On the following day, a transport was due to head north to the coast. The new master of the King's horses had arranged for it to stop off at Bathar. Nakht was going home to see his family, on leave of absence. The victory festival was a great success. Many Thebans compared it to Amenhotep III's Heb-Sed celebrations. These were held every three years, following the thirtieth year of a Pharaoh's reign, and were meant to signify renewal of the King. But few people present, especially the priests of Karnak, were left in any doubt that this festival day celebrated only one person: Amenhotep IV. Ay on the other hand, considered the day to be his own personal triumph. He had advanced his own cause and that of his young protégée. And his arch enemy at court, Ramose had been forced to watch in silence at his promotion to high office. The office of Vizier and Governor of Thebes was a job that Ay had in his sights. Not that it was the limit of his ambitions. In his mind, he had a long way to go beyond that.

Chapter Eight

Admiral Habt's ship made good progress up the Nile, on the second day of the journey to Thebes. The North wind filled the vessel's sails and carried the ship and its company south. Because of the strong wind neither the sailors or the soldiers were required to man the oars. Before the ship had cast off its moorings, Nakht and his men had bathed in the river. While they had done so, one of the crew had kept a watch out for crocodiles. It felt good to lose the dust and dirt of the desert, which was secured to the skin by the very sweat from a man's body. Then as they ate a breakfast of fresh fruit and bread, washed down with weak beer, the boat had set sail. Once again the Admiral took charge of piloting the ship. Nakht's words from the previous night were fresh in the Admiral's mind. It seemed that the soldier's mission had been a success, but the grand Vizier was still going to be angry. So it was in his own best interests to keep the vessel moving swiftly. That way Lord Ay's anger might be deflected towards the army rather than the navy – and away from himself in particular.

The prevailing wind left Nakht with little to do. He had almost looked forward to taking a turn with the oars. Ever since his first boat journey with Ay and Horemheb, he had enjoyed sailing up and down the river. And making himself useful, while afloat, was something that he had always had enjoyed doing. Feeling at a loose end, he sought out Djar and asked him to bring the Hittite's severed hand. After the ambush it had been covered in sand and wrapped in layers of bandages. Then it had been put in a linen bag, which by now was attracting the attention of various flies. Nakht looked at the linen bag and decided against unwrapping and washing the trophy at this stage. That job could be done after they arrived in Thebes, in time for Ay to present it to his bride. Having unnecessarily satisfied himself that the hand was safe, he dismissed Djar and sat at the side of the boat. He relaxed and watched the ship's hull glide effortlessly through the water. *Just like he had done on his return to Bathar, after the victory celebrations in Thebes...*

...Nakht was very apprehensive on the journey down river to Bathar. It had been almost three years since he had seen his family. Once he had learned how to write, he had sent them letters, knowing that a scribe would eventually appear in the village to read them out to his father. But he had received nothing back. Many times the youth had also prayed to Amun, seeking reassurance that his family were well. Although he wasn't only concerned about his family's well being. In the intervening years since his departure, he also worried that they might have forgotten about him. Possibly they would not want to know him any more. Nakht was also sure that they wouldn't even recognise him. Physically, he had developed since moving to Thebes. He was not only taller and broader, but his voice was now much deeper. As the naval, transport vessel approached his village, a large part of Nakht wished that he was still in Thebes, attending upon Ay. He swallowed heavily and tugged at his amulet, where he kept the King's Gold of Honour, out of nervousness.

The transport's captain insisted on berthing the ship, so that his passenger could disembark in style. Nakht would have been happy to jump over the side of the boat and swim ashore. This was because the sight of such an impressive vessel had drawn a crowd of onlookers. Boats of this size did not moor in Bathar. So the village came to a halt and approached his landing place. As he left the ship, its captain assured him that another vessel would collect him for the homeward journey two days after the moon rose. He thanked the naval officer and clambered onto dry land to face the people from his childhood. Glancing at the crowd, he thought that he could make out several familiar faces. But their wary expressions told him clearly that they could not place him. It was obvious that the villagers did not know what to make of this tall young man from the big boat. Even his clean linen kilt and leather sandals set him apart from them. Eventually, he broke the rather awkward silence by saying, "I'm Nakht...don't any of you remember me? I've returned from Thebes to see my family."

Nakht...Nakht...the word was repeated several times by the crowd. Then one of the older men shouted, "It's Hapu's son. The one who was carried away on a chariot, by that stranger from Thebes. I thought that he'd been dead for years!"

Suddenly their expressions changed. He was one of their own. Not a tax collector or a another such official, who could only cause them trouble. Several came forwards and slapped him on the back. The man who had identified him as Hapu's son said, "You're looking very prosperous, young man. It looks like you've done well for yourself in Thebes!"

Nakht recognised him as Menna, a fisherman. He replied, "I've done my best and tried not to let anyone down."

"Good for you, son – I'm sure you've done us proud. Now, let me take you to your father. It's no use going to your old house. Your family has a much bigger place now, in keeping with their importance to the community..."

Menna led him through the crowd to the edge of the village to what, by Bathar's standards, was an impressive house. The fishermen yelled, by way announcement, "Hapu and Ese, come quickly. Your oldest son is home to see you!"

Before long several of Nakht's bothers and sisters came running out of the house. When they saw the tall stranger, standing next to Menna, they stopped in their tracks, unsure as to who he was. But at least his mother recognised him. She screamed and hugged him tightly. Before she even released her grip, she had a hundred questions, all fired out one after another. Finally, she took his hand and escorted him into the family home telling him,
"This is your house son. Your father built it with the money that the stranger gave him that day..."

"Where is he?" Nakht asked, anxious to see his father.

"At the temple. Now that your father is a wealthy man he has many duties to perform for the good of our village. Today he is consulting with the priests."

Hapu returned shortly before the sun went down. His welcome was much more restrained than Ese's, but none the less joyful. Dinner was a long meal that night, as Nakht's brothers and sisters asked him question after question. Had he seen the Pharaoh? Was the Queen as beautiful as people said she was? Had he fought in a battle? Did the people of Thebes never rise until the sun reached its mid point? The list just went on and on. Like himself, they were all much bigger than they had been three years ago. There had been no new additions to the family, since his departure. He was pleased to see that his mother and father had not aged dramatically since then. If anything, his father's new role in the village seemed to have given him a renewed lease of life. His mother too, seemed less stressed or worried than he remembered her to be. When the meal was finally over, Hapu sent his younger children and his wife to bed. Then he placed a jug of strong beer on the table and said, "It is really good to see you son. There's barely a day that passes when I don't think about you. I never worry, because I receive your letters. These days the priests read them to me for free! I don't have to wait for itinerant scribes to appear!"

Nakht answered, "Forgive me, but why didn't you send word back to me? It would have set my mind at rest."

Hapu nodded, before saying, "I knew you'd ask that question. It's difficult to answer…but when I first received your letters I was proud. Written by my own son, one scribes said with real admiration in his voice. Well, I decided there and then that I would learn to read and write, before I sent a letter to you. That is why I spend so much time at the temple. In return for large donations, the priests are teaching me to read and write!"

They both laughed at this, as Hapu poured out two beakers of ale. Then he went onto relate how his life had changed since Nakht had departed. Using the two bars of gold, he had built the new house and bought land. Hapu now had people working for him and only farmed or fished when he chose to. He had also become the headman of the village. This was due to the influence that his wealth had brought him with the priests. Just as it was in Karnak, generous religious offerings bought preference. Then it was Nakht's turn to talk. He explained everything about his life in Thebes, from the moment he had left Bathar. With some shame he related how he had come to receive the King's Gold of Honour. But his father's reaction surprised him, when he said, "Lord Ay was right, son. Let people believe something happened and it did. Besides, what chance did this family have before Ay arrived in the village and took a shine to you. Not one of those bloody scribes would even give us the time of day. The priests would barely acknowledge me back then and now they tutor me. Stick with your master, boy!"

The month in Bathar passed slowly. Apart from helping his father, with his reading and writing, there was little for him to do. The family's fields were tended by their workers. His father took him fishing every couple of days, but Nakht was bored. By the end of the second week he was desperate to return to Thebes. Now that he was sure that his family were well and prospering, the youth wanted to get back to his military training. It was with some relief that he eventually boarded the return transport and sailed south. But back in Thebes Ay had some disconcerting news for him. As a recipient of the King's gold he could not return to the barracks. It would be improper for him to train with soldiers after receiving such an honour. Instead he was sent back to the Chief Scribe's office, to study military treatises. In the Pharaoh's library, he read and re-read everything about the campaigns of Amose and Tuthmosis III. And that was how Nakht spent the next couple of years, until he was turned seventeen.

Shortly after his seventeenth anniversary, Aye took him to one side and told him that his work in the Chief Scribe's office was over. It was time for him to return to practical matters. There had been an increased spate of tomb robbing, in the Valley of the Kings, on the west bank close to Thebes. Ay had arranged for him to be seconded to the force that patrolled the valley at night. Tomb robbing was a very serious matter. It was not just a question of the theft of funerary offerings. More often than not the thieves would go onto burn a sarcophagus, to detach the gold leaf from it. This act destroyed the mummified body of the unfortunate dead ruler. And no body on earth meant death for the Pharaoh in the afterlife. The reason for Nakht's secondment was that Ay had been informed that the

Valley's guards were being bribed by the robbers. So he planned to send Nakht in undercover to see if there was any truth in these rumours. Both knew that the work could and probably would be dangerous. But Nakht now looked to be almost twenty and was nearly a foot taller than Ay. And the Commander of the King's horse, after consulting Bast, believed it to be time for the youth's next test. Besides Ramose had already failed to put a halt to the desecrations. He'd had his chance. Now it was Ay's turn to show the Pharaoh just who he could trust to get a job done.

Chapter Nine

Nakht was dragged back to present and the Nile transport by Djar shaking his shoulder. His body stiffened and jerked, as he snapped out of his thoughts. The second in command moved back a pace and said apologetically, "I'm very sorry to disturb you, sir. But there was no reply when I spoke to you. The Admiral has just arranged for lunch to be served. Will you be eating?"

"I might as well, as there is nothing else for me to do." He followed Djar to the makeshift mess, where his men were stuffing themselves with cold meat. Nakht toyed with his food, eating no more than a few mouthfuls. To his regret it was far too early in the day to ask for some red wine. So he made do with the cloudy beer which the Admiral's men had served with their food. After lunch he had a brief conversation with Habt, purely out of courtesy. Nakht was experienced enough to know that the wind was still holding in their favour. The voyage was going well and they were speeding through the water. After reminding the naval officer that his men were ready to take the oars, should the wind fall, he returned to his berth. *Once he was seated, it was only a short journey to recall his time on patrol in the Valley of the Kings...*

...Ay had instructed him not to put his life at risk. But he also told him that Amenhotep IV wanted no more of his deceased relatives to be incinerated. How this was to be done, if Nakht found himself heavily outnumbered, was not explained. According to Ay, this was to be left to the young man's discretion. He decided that the better part of discretion was to be well armed. So on his first night of duty he turned up with sword, dagger and spear. The watch's leader Harkhaf, a

small man in his mid thirties, knew nothing about Nakht, being from the civil guard. As far as he was concerned, their new recruit was a farm boy. He had been allocated to this duty by the authorities. Obviously Harkhaf was smart enough smell a rat. It wouldn't be the first time that an informer had been placed in their midst. But Nakht's tattered apron and slow ambling gait was enough to allay his initial suspicions. Even his weaponry was nothing out of the ordinary. All the guards were issued with such arms. The darkness prevented his "comrades" from seeing that the blades of Nakht's sword and dagger were the finest that the Egyptian empire could currently manufacture.

For over two weeks Nakht trudged around the valley at night with his new comrades. When he was spoken to, he replied in the accent that he knew from his childhood in Bathar. Each patrol had four members and they worked every night. Ay had placed him in the detail that was under the most suspicion. But to complicate his position even further, Nakht had been informed that merely implicating the patrol was not enough. The Pharaoh wanted the gang of tomb robbers that they were colluding with as well. When Nakht was off duty, he ran various possibilities through his mind, thinking of ways that he could achieve his aims. Although all this did was to keep him awake. Eventually, he gave up thinking and decided that he would just have to take his chance - if it ever came.

This finally happened at the end of his third week of guard duties. The patrol was heading north, towards the Valley of the Kings and had just passed Deir Al-Medina. It was the first of several sweeps of the area which they made each night. The slightly built Harkhaf, took him to one side and whispered, "Farm boy, don't you get fed up of working for fresh air? Every night we trudge up and down this valley. And for what?"

Nakht hesitated, to stifle the butterflies in his stomach, before replying,
"I don't really know. To be honest, I've had since arriving in Thebes has been my food and lodgings..."

"Exactly!" Harkhaf interrupted, "Now listen. I've been watching you since the day that you joined my patrol. And I think you're on the level. Suppose I told you that we could make some real money. It might be a bit risky. But you could go back home a wealthy man when your duty finishes!"

"What...what would I have to do?"

"Just lend a hand to a few friends of mine. They'll do all the hard work. We just help out and pretend that we never saw them. Then in a couple of weeks you'll get your share. Are you with us, lad?"

There could be no answer other than yes. Even if he were not undercover, Nakht would have had to say yes. "No" would have meant a dagger in the back. Harkhaf's four "friends" were waiting for him close to the place where the trail forked. Right took you to Deir Al-Bahri and left towards the tombs of the New Kingdom Pharaohs. In silence they took the left fork and started to climb. The tombs were cut deep into the rock face. Some descended several hundred feet below ground level. They all had disguised entrances to hide their location, which themselves could be hundreds of feet above ground level. But the robbers would have been tipped off, by some discontented building worker or official. They knew exactly where they were heading and had come equipped to do their job. In the moonlight, Nakht could see that they had ropes, picks and even kindling. The latter was required to start a fire underneath the stone sarcophagus, to melt its gold lining.

The group continued to ascend the narrow trail for some time. Finally the leader of the robbers raised his hand to halt the part. Moving forwards towards the edge of the cliff face, he took his bearings in the moonlight. Pointing towards a large rock, he indicated that they had arrived. Straight away, the gang drove four large wooden pegs into cracks in the rock, some six feet from the cliff's edge. Then two ropes were firmly tied to the pegs, before their other end was secured around the waists of two gang members. In the darkness, the men gradually lowered themselves over edge and began their descent to the tomb's suspected entrance. Nakht had originally been detailed to pay out one of the ropes. But he told Harkhaf that he was unable to stand close to the cliff's edge, due to a fear of heights. So he was given a large rock and told to keep an eye on the pegs, tamping them down from time to time.

    The youth was still unsure as to what to do about the imminent desecration. But he admired the courage and ingenuity of the thieves. Lowering themselves down a cliff at night took some guts. Soon he heard a gentle tapping sound rising up from below. It sounded as if the entrance had been located and the man made plaster was being chipped away. The robbers worked swiftly until they had established a foothold in the false rock face. When the ropes went limp, it was obvious that they had successfully entered the tomb. Their two colleagues pulled the ropes up, secured themselves and descended the cliff. Nakht was concentrating on ensuring that the wooden pegs were in place, when an idea came to him. The odds against him had just been reduced from seven to one, to three to one. And if he could move quickly then they would come down even further. Nakht glanced up to see Harkhaf supervising the two other members of the patrol, who had not finished lowering the second pair of robbers. Rising to his feet he whispered as loud as he dared, "Quickly,

Master...please. I've got a problem with one of the pegs. It's split, come and look..."

Harkhaf quietly told the other two men to be extra careful and came over to Nakht. The youth gestured in the direction of the pegs. Then as the smaller man crouched, to inspect the non-existent damage, he stood behind him. In an instant he swung his right hand, which was holding the good sized rock, towards the side of the watch commander's face. It connected and Harkhaf was knocked into silent oblivion. As he crumpled to the ground, Nakht approached the other two members of the patrol. They were still stood with their backs to him, carefully letting the ropes out.

"Harkhaf is repairing the peg," he hissed, receiving only a grunt in acknowledgement. Then the moment he had anticipated arrived. The ropes went limp – the second pair robbers had entered the tomb. Anxious to take a moment's respite, the two men let the ropes drop. Relieved of their heavy burden, the guards sighed with relief. Nakht said nothing. Instead he yawned and outstretched his arms with one movement. His second movement was to push his hands forward quickly, into the men's backs. Caught off guard and relaxed, they were propelled forwards. With their balance lost they toppled over the edge of the cliff, yelling loudly as they fell. Before they had time to crash into the valley floor, Nakht had hauled the ropes up. With the four tomb robbers now trapped, some two hundred feet above the ground, the odds were most definitely in his favour. The youth walked back over to Harkhaf. He was still lying unconscious at the side of the pegs. Nakht bound his hands and feet securely and then went off to summon help. He wished that Pteti, his old adversary from the training ground, had been there to watch him hit Harkhaf. Then he could have seen the correct way of laying a man out.

To say that Ay was pleased with his actions would be an understatement. In his opinion Nakht was getting better and better. The fact that the captain of horse had succeeded, where others had failed the Pharaoh, was at the forefront of Ay's thoughts. As a reward to his protégé, he invited Nakht to attend the trial of the surviving conspirators. Such trials were attended by the King himself. Robbing a royal tomb was the most heinous offence that an Egyptian could commit. Although on this occasion, the thieves had been very unlucky on more than being caught. The tomb they had entered was empty. It had been carved and sealed to act as a decoy for unwitting robbers. And for once a decoy tomb had done its job. But there were only three survivors left to face justice. In Nakht's absence, while he was summoning assistance, two of the robbers had fallen to their deaths. They had been attempting to scale the cliff's face without ropes.

Four days after their arrest the three surviving thieves were brought before Amenhotep and Nefertiti at Malkata. Following his disagreement with the priesthood, the Pharaoh had halted the practice of trying such criminals at the temple of Monthu in Karnak. As always, the royal couple were accompanied by the grand Vizier Ramose. He stood at the side of the Pharaoh and conspicuously avoided making any eye contact with Ay. Nakht also noticed that Harkhaf still appeared to be quite groggy from the blow that he had delivered. All three were led into the courtyard and securely tied to a raised tables. This was so that the Kings guard could beat their feet with rods, to extract their confessions. Nakht found the spectacle slightly distasteful, but thought to himself that the men would have known the risks that they were taking. After around thirty minutes the names of their informants were revealed. Shortly after that, a full list of their crimes was obtained. While the beatings were taking place both the Pharaoh and his great wife watched with interest. When all the useful information had been thrashed out of the thieves, Amenhotep pronounced sentence. Death by impalement. This mandatory punishment was why two Of the robbers had preferred to die, while trying to escape from the tomb.

The Pharaoh's guard removed the men's bonds and helped them to their badly bruised feet. They were then dragged out of the palace's grounds to a nearby field. Three thick wooden stakes with sharp points had already been placed in the earth. One by one, the three condemned men's hands and feet were bound. Then facing downwards, they were carefully lowered onto the three feet pieces of wood. The guards ensured that the tip of the point was pressed up against their stomachs. Next, each man was given a gentle shove in the back by a guard. This was to help him on his way, by ensuring that the wooden point pierced the flesh and entered his belly. Finally the guards stood back and let the men's body weight patiently do its work. Inch by painful inch, and unable to resist in any way, the helpless criminals' momentum forced them further down onto the stakes. When the tip of the wooden point came through their backs most of the guards departed. Only the most hardened and sadistic remained to watch the tomb robbers' loud and agonisingly slow deaths.

Away from all of this, in the palace courtyard, Amenhotep awarded Nakht the King's Gold of Honour for the second time announcing, "For one so young to prevail over seven men deserves reward. For the last three nights, both myself and my departed relatives have slept peacefully."

And just like the first time he had received the award, Nakht was unable to take his eyes off Nefertiti. Ay, who was stood proudly at the youth's side, saw this.

But he also noticed that his daughter's gaze was also fixed upon Nakht's well developed young body. It was something to commit to his memory. Something that he might be able put to good use one day. In the meantime, he decided to actively promote the third strand of the Nakht's legend. To Ay's devious mind, "The Marsh Boy who slew seven tomb robbers" had a poetic ring to it. At least the epithet might deter other thieves, while furthering the prestige of his own endeavours to the detriment of Ramose's.

Chapter Ten

On board Admiral Habt's transport, the afternoon of the second day passed as slowly as the morning. Several times, Nakht paced the foredeck out of sheer boredom and restlessness. Due to the lack of red wine, his body had started to sweat – as the withdrawal symptoms set in. He needed something stronger than the weak beer which had accompanied their lunch. When the sun started to dip in the sky, he called Djar over. With only a hint of shame, he sent him to acquire a pitcher of wine. The second in command knew all about his superior's taste for drink. He was constantly amazed at Nakht's capacity for alcohol and the fact that he never seemed to get drunk. When Djar returned with a clay vessel, which was almost filled to the brim, Nakht sent him on his way. Then he returned to his seat by the unmanned oars in the bow. Several gulps of red wine later, *he returned again to his early years of service to Ay...*

...who had decided that Nakht should not marry. In Egyptian society it was normal for a man to take a wife between the ages of sixteen and twenty. Nakht was now turned nineteen. But in the two years following his second award of the Pharaoh's Gold, Ay had actively discouraged him from seeking out suitable female companions. The captain of the King's horses gave him permission to satisfy his sexual urges, but only with low status women. Although several respectable families had suggested offers of marriage, Ay had rebuffed them. He had assured Nakht that far greater things lay on their joint horizons, than just a wife and children. As Ay was his guardian and mentor, the young man deferred to his will. Overall, it had been a very strange two years which followed his success in

capturing the tomb robbers. The Pharaoh's father, Amenhotep III, had finally been given relief from his paralysing toothaches and passed on to the next world. He had been buried in the Valley of Kings, in a secret tomb.

During these confused years, Nakht had often found himself at a loose end. Egypt had no foreign wars to fight, so much of the army had been disbanded. Also, there was no way that he could be return to patrolling the Valley of the Kings. He was now far too well known for bringing the tomb robbers to justice. Even the Chief Scribe's office was barred to him. Ay had decided that such studies could teach him nothing further. So he spent most days in attendance at Ay's shoulder, in the King's court. It was not something that he enjoyed. The bickering and wrangling of senior courtiers, especially between Ay and Ramose, irritated him. But when the King was present the arguments ceased. Then, all they seemed to do was to agree with everything Amenhotep said, in a more obsequious manner than the previous courtier, who had also just agreed whole heartedly with the Pharaoh. But from Nakht's perspective there was one advantage of attending court. Nefertiti often accompanied her husband to these sessions. And when she was present, gazing down upon everyone like a divine manifestation on earth, Nakht found that the time flew by.

But now that he was approaching adulthood, and had acquired greater comprehension, the Pharaoh's behaviour started to stroke him as odd. To begin with the King's long running dispute with the Karnak priesthood suddenly escalated. Amenhotep began the fight by excluding them from his court at Malkarta. And when he crossed the river to the eastern bank, he would only attend his father's temple to Ma'att in Luxor. He refused to venture as far north as the religious complex at Karnak. Which was only two miles away and no distance at all to be carried by his servants. Then he began to promulgate his belief in the Aten, at every available opportunity. It was almost as if Amun had ceased to exist or matter. Amenhotep even ordered the construction of a temple to the Aten. To the annoyance of the priests, it was built by the east gate of Amun's temple at Karnak. Nakht was unsure as to whether the King was a great visionary or a complete madman. And when he made these religious pronouncements, Nefertiti was at his side. Her eyes sometimes met Nakht's, albeit briefly. For some reason, the youth imagined those soft brown eyes promising him something that could never be delivered or acted upon.

In private, Ay enlightened Nakht about the purpose of the new religion. The worship of Amun and all the other gods was finished – as were their various priesthoods. From now on only the Aten, the great solar disc, was to be worshipped. And he could only be approached by Amenhotep IV. Although it later emerged that Nefertiti was to be considered a member of this unique priesthood of just two people. But in compensation, all of the King's subjects could enjoy the beneficial warmth of the Aten's rays. Unlike the hidden deities, under the old religion, this made worshipping the Aten more inclusive. The Aten was Re the sun god – but with his body removed. So all that remained was his head or the solar disc. Under the new order, only the Pharaoh could intercede with the Aten to avert chaos. Everyone else could worship Amenhotep rather than the multitude of gods who had previously received their prayers. So now there was no need for a priesthood to approach the gods on anyone's behalf. In one stroke, the King had removed his ancestors' devolvement of the power of intercession from the priests. They were all redundant and their temples' wealth, accordingly belonged to the Pharaoh. In Ay's considered opinion it was a recipe for disaster. Very few people in Egypt had Amenhotep's vision or madness. Most would be reluctant to exchange the solar disc for the gods that had been worshipped for thousands of years.

In response to objections from the priests of Karnak, Memphis and Heliopolis Amenhotep IV decided to fan the flames. The Pharaoh was in no mood to seek a compromise. Firstly, he renamed himself Akhenaten, or the servant of the Aten. Secondly, Nefertiti was renamed as Nefer-Nefru-Aten – one who is beautiful in the sight of the Aten. To compound matters he declared his mother, Amenhotep III's great wife, Queen Tiy to be a living god. This was something that was unheard of for the Queen of a dead ruler. And just when the priesthood might have been sufficiently enraged, Akhenaten started to travel the Kingdom. He had tired of Thebes and was looking for a site to build a new political and religious capital. Ay, who until now had gone with the flow, took a few moments to stand back and reflect. The Commander of the King's horse saw only see trouble ahead. But he could handle trouble, provided it was on his own terms. So he used all his influence to have Nakht placed in charge of Queen Nefer-Nefru-Aten's bodyguard. In the continued absence of the Pharaoh, she would need protecting. And there was nobody better fitted to the job than the firm, muscled young man, whom she was constantly gazing upon at court.

Nakht had passed his twentieth birthday before he took command of Nefertiti's guard. He refused to think of her by her new name. Not only was it too long, it grated on his nerves. In his opinion, she was beautiful to everyone. Not just the Aten. Her husband eventually found the site for the new capital, north of Thebes on the eastern bank of the Nile. In a virgin site, which he named Akhetaten or the horizon of the Aten, the new city was founded. In time it became better known as Tel Al-Armana. The construction of the city in the desert became Akhenaten's prevailing passion. Although Nefertiti journeyed on occasions to their new home, Nakht saw that she lacked her husband's enthusiasm for the project. He was also aware that the tide of political and social opinion was turning against Akhenaten. Behind his back, the Karnak priesthood had been doing their worst. According to them the Pharaoh was a heretic and Nefertiti was a demon from the underworld. Her deadly witchcraft had caused the King to disown the true gods. Nakht dismissed such blatant and ignorant propaganda. But he could understand why so many people were confused and angry. All their lives they had worshipped Amun-Re and now, by decree of their Pharaoh, it had to stop.

After several months in his new role, which alternated between Thebes and Armana, Nakht became better acquainted with the Queen. He always maintained a respectful distance and asked no favours. She was affable to him and he was always polite in conversation to Nefertiti. Her father Lord Ay was his patron and he sought no other. But his patron, on the other hand, was playing a far more devious game. His stock had risen in the court, threatening the position of Ramose. The old Vizier now spent more time supervising the building of his tomb in Thebes than on matters of state. And by throwing his protégée and his daughter together Ay hoped that in the absence of Akhenaten nature would take its course. When that happened he would have a further hold over his daughter, the Queen. It would also strengthen his hold over the young man whom he had taken into his household, eight years earlier. Either way, Ay knew that he was in a position where he could not possibly lose.

It took nature six months to run its course. Despite Nakht's devotion to duty and service, his continued attendance on the Queen took its toll on his resolve. When he was on duty he could not keep his eyes off her. But that was better than when he was off duty, when things were even worse. Then he couldn't stop thinking about Nefertiti and longed to be in her presence. Sometimes his body ached so much to be with her, that it hurt him physically. So it was great trepidation that he responded to her personal summons, one summer morning. Akhenaten had been away for a month supervising the building at Armana. Nefertiti had refused to travel across the desert, because of the heat, preferring to spend her time at the palace of Malkata. When Nakht reached her chambers he was mortified to see that she had dismissed her maids and that they were alone together.

Nefertiti was still in bed. As Nakht entered the room, she pulled the bedclothes around her neck and smiled at him. Unsure as to what to say he stood in attendance, staring at his feet. The Queen seemed to take pleasure in his discomfort, because she smiled and said, "So, now you are unable to look at me. This is not normally the case. Usually your eyes are fixed to my body..."

As Nefertiti's voice tailed off she climbed out of the bed. Nakht swallowed heavily because she was completely naked. Her slender, olive body gave him an instant erection. The Queen walked over to him and placed her hands on his shoulders, pressing her crutch against his thigh. Until then he had barely noticed her delicately shaved pubenda. Gently her hand caressed his crotch and she sighed with both pleasure and anticipation. Nakht half backed way from her, which brought that sensual smile back to her face. Nefertiti looked him in the eyes before saying, "As your Queen, I order you to take your kilt off. I want to see the big fat cock that you are hiding beneath it!" Her hands were now running up and down his firm stomach and she was breathing very heavily.

"But my lady...surely this is very dangerous...?"

"Shut up and give me your cock. I want you to take me now, not in a week's time!" As Nefertiti replied, her hands were busy in the act of tearing his kilt off. When that was done, she pushed Nakht onto the bed and took him in her mouth. This made him feel very aroused and immediately close to his orgasm. Although before he could ejaculate she took his penis out of her mouth and mounted him, his stiff cock sliding easily into her tight, moist cunt.. With a supreme effort of willpower, Nakht held himself back until Nefertiti reached her peak. Then he carried on thrusting and sucking at her tiny breasts. Just before the moment before when he was ready to release his fluids, she pulled herself off him. Nakht moaned with frustration as his member throbbed and his orgasm ebbed away. But Nefertiti did not leave him to suffer for long. Grasping him firmly with her firm right hand, she drained the soldier of his load, which he sprayed all over the Queen and her bed sheets. As Nakht spurted, he cried out loudly, in an absolute ecstasy that he had never known before. When his ejaculation was completed, Nefertiti relinquished her grip and said to him jovially, "I do like my soldiers to stand to attention. Especially when they are big boys like yourself..."

Then in a moment her tone changed, as she continued, "But Nakht, you must listen to me. There is more for two of us to enjoy – much more. Although, you must be aware that my father will know about us. His spies are everywhere. So if he asks you about us, just deny everything. He will have no proof. These bed sheets will be destroyed this afternoon!"

"But what about your husband, the King?" Nakht asked.

"Because of his new religion, he wouldn't notice if the whole of the Egyptian army lined up and fucked me, one man after another. We have not made love since his crusade against the priests started." Then she noticed that Nakht was still hard and gently climbed back on top of him. Nefertiti kissed him passionately on his lips, before reaching behind herself for his penis. Despite the Queen's words of warning, he did not object to her renewed advances in the slightest. His wildest fantasies were being fulfilled, by the most beautiful woman in the civilised world.

Chapter Eleven

The second night on the Nile transport was identical to the first. As the sun set, Admiral Habt's sailors moored the vessel and prepared the evening meal. By now the crew needed no prompting from Djar to keep Nakht's pitcher topped up with wine. But if the Admiral had thought that a generous supply of alcohol would loosen the soldier's tongue, he was wrong. Over dinner, Nakht rebuffed even attempts to make polite conversation, let alone respond to any questions relating to the grand Vizier. Habt could understand how Nakht had obtained the soubriquet of the silent assassin. When the meal was over Nakht retired to the foredeck, with his blanket and his drink. He had decided to spend the night in the open. This was mainly due to the hammock, which was getting on his nerves. Because of his great height, it was far too small for him. He was always half in and half out of it. At least he could stretch out to his fullest extent on the wooden deck. *And think about the great love of his life – Nefertiti...*

...In the course of their affair, it soon became obvious that she was being driven to distraction by the King. She told Nakht that he was pot bellied freak, who was the product of too much interbreeding in the royal family. This was something that Nakht had often wondered about. The bloodline of the Pharaohs and the Kingship itself passed through the female side of the royal house. An heir apparent, could only become Pharaoh by effectively marrying back into his own family. It was not unknown for brother to marry sister to secure accession to the throne. Ay had explained to him that steps were taken by the royal family to limit potential damage. More often than not, a half brother would marry a half sister rather than a full sibling.

Nefertiti had brought fresh blood into the dynasty, being the daughter of a commoner – Ay. But the future of her bloodline was at risk. Although she was the great King's wife, she was not the mother of the crown prince. That honour belonged to Kiya, a minor wife who had given birth to a boy called Tutankhaten or the living image of the Aten. Unlike Kiya, Nefertiti had only given Akhenaten daughters. There was no guarantee that any of them would be chosen as the young prince's bride.

In the sixth year of Akhenaten's reign the royal family and household left Thebes for the last time. They moved to the newly completed palace at Armana. Nakht was now twenty one years old and his affair with Nefertiti had been going on for over a year. Ay was aware of their intimacy, but kept his own counsel while it suited him. He was now approaching fifty years of age but judged events to be moving in his favour. His great rival Ramose had died earlier in the year and the King was increasingly relying upon Ay's advice. It helped that he had enthusiastically embraced the new religion. In the presence of the Pharaoh, at least, Ay worshipped the Aten devoutly. Horemheb had also continued his progression in the army. He now held the rank of captain in the Kings guard, like Ay before him. But although Nakht remained in charge of the Queen's guard, Ay soon found him other work to do.

The older man's earlier premonition about Egypt's lack of enthusiasm for Akhenaten's brand of monotheism proved to be well founded. This was especially the case in Thebes, where the old religion was so firmly rooted. The worship of Amun could not be completely eradicated, especially in private. But Akhenaten had decided that it would not be tolerated in public. At his command, gangs of stonemasons were sent out to Egypt's major temples. They were instructed to remove all references to the old gods. In practice this meant chiselling away their hieroglyphs from a temple's columns and walls. And given the resistance of the priesthood and populace, the gangs needed the protection of armed men. Nakht found himself in charge of ensuring the workmen's safety at Karnak.

These escort missions always met with violent opposition from the local people people of Thebes. While the soldiers were present the priests were nowhere near the site of dissent. But prior to their arrival, the priesthood had previously stirred up trouble with the rabble. Then they sat back and let the populace bear the brunt of the Pharaoh's displeasure. Nakht had noticed this, having carried out several missions of this sort. By this stage of his life, he was beginning to be disillusioned with religion. Whether it was old or new. At the age of twenty one he had personally killed or caused the death of eight men. He was also sleeping with the King's great wife. In his mind, Nakht had decided that when the time came to face Osiris, his own fate was sealed. He had not and probably would not ever lead a just life. The afterlife, in the fields of Yaru, was already closed to him. So he had no qualms about rigidly enforcing Ay's instructions.

The fourth strand of his legend was born on his fifth visit to Karnak temple. He had a gang of ten masons and the same number of soldiers under his command. As he was now permanently based in Armana the journey to Thebes took several day's travel. It was more than enough time for the priests' spies to warn them of his impending arrival. So whenever he arrived at Karnak the entrance to the temple was blocked by protesters His detail had to beat the local people out of the way to gain entrance to the temple. Sometimes the injuries that they inflicted were quite severe. Cracked skulls or limbs were not unknown. Prior to this mission, he had sought out Ay's guidance.

Nakht was sick to his hind teeth of the priests causing trouble and then letting others suffer the consequences. Ay had weighed the matter up and decided that the Pharaoh might not mind a little clerical bloodshed. He authorised Nakht to do as he saw fit when he was in Karnak.

To start with, the fifth mission was no different to any other. The soldiers escorted the workmen into the temple, wielding their wooden staffs upon the crowd. There were a great many shouts of ,"Go back to your heretic King in Armana" or "Leave Amun be and slay the evil witch". These slogans were intermingled with cries of pain, as the soldier's staves did their work and opened up a path. Once they were safely inside the temple, the workmen started on their work. But as they started to chisel away at the columns in the great courtyard a junior priest emerged from the darkness of the hypostyle (or pillared) hall. He was a slight, young man who was not much older than Nakht. This was all part of what the soldier called the desecration ritual. The High Priest would send an acolyte to warn the workmen about incurring the wrath of Amun-Re. The soldiers and workers would ignore the warning and continue their work. But on this occasion Nakht had decided that he would take the matter further. So when the young priest had delivered his warning he said, "I have a warning of my own for your master. Take me to him!"

The emissary shuddered and shook his head saying, "You may not enter the sanctuary...it is not allowed. You are..."

"Unclean," Nakht interjected, "But I know that already. So return to your sanctuary and I will follow. I personally mean you no harm, but it is time for me to have my say, to your master!"

The acolyte saw Nakht's hand caress the hilt of his curved sword. He also saw the serious expression on the young officer's face. His nerve deserted him completely and he set off for the innermost sanctum of the temple at a quick pace. Leaving the courtyard, he disappeared into the darkness of the hypostyle hall's tall columns. But Nakht's long legs enabled him to keep pace without any undue effort. Eventually, they emerged from the columns and arrived at the entrance to the sanctuary. The young priest knew that Nakht was almost on his shoulder. But he still ran into one of the rooms at the rear of the temple crying, "Holiness, please forgive me. I did not seek to betray you, this man followed me!"

There were twenty priests in the room, huddled together. Nakht saw that their privations were not entirely uncomfortable – they had fine wines and good food for company. The room was well lit by candles and torchlight. One of their number, an old man, rose to his feet and said, "How dare you enter this holy place! Only the sacred priests of Amun-Re are permitted to enter this far into the temple."

Nakht's face showed that he was less than convinced with this argument. He recognised the thin old man, with piercing eyes, from the day of the expedition's departure for Kush. It was the first priest of Amun. Nakht answered, "Every time that I follow the King's instructions, you send me a warning. Now you will listen to mine. Stop rousing the people of Thebes to the point of insurrection. It is they that feel our rods rather than yourselves. But that will shortly change if you do not listen to my words."

Having delivered his warning Nakht turned to depart. But the High Priest was not prepared to be spoken to in such a way. He walked over to Nakht and pushed him roughly in the back before saying, "Your words are like yourself. They are an empty threat to me. I can call on Amun to strike you down at a moment's notice. Do you really want me to do that?" Nakht turned to face him and drew his sword. He was angry, but tried to maintain his composure. After staring directly at the High Priest he said,

"Very well. Let us make a wager and see if your god is stronger than my sword arm. Do your worst and call upon him – I am ready to take the consequences. But are you?"

The High Priest of Karnak suddenly sensed the danger that he was in and swallowed, heavily. But he also saw the faces of his fellow priests. If he ducked this challenge, their respect for his leadership would be lost forever. So he raised his head and hands upwards and cried, "Amun-Re greatest of all the gods! I, your humble servant, call upon you for assistance. Strike this heretic, who has invaded your holiest place, from the face of this earth…"

The other priests initially rubbed their hands together, at the prospect of Amun's divine intervention. But when they saw that Nakht was still standing, after the exhortation to Amun, their expressions changed. But not as much as the High Priest's, when the soldier said to him, "Your excretory spells are a little rusty and do not appear to be working today. My blade, however, is always sharp…"

In one movement Nakht raised his sword and brought it crashing down into the old man's neck. Blood spurted everywhere from his jugular vein. The High Priest was dead before he hit the tiled floor. His colleagues maintained their seated positions, not wanting to risk suffering the same fate. Nakht glanced down at the dead man and said to them, "Remember my words about stirring up trouble in Thebes. Nobody is above the King's command!"

Then he retraced his steps to the great courtyard, where he spent the rest of the day watching the workmen deface the carvings of Amun.

When Ay heard about this incident he was overjoyed. For some months he had thought that Nakht had gone soft, because of his relationship with Nefertiti. But to slaughter the High Priest of Karnak, in front of his minions, showed him that his boy was back to top form. It was the first time that a senior priest, from a major temple, had been killed in the course of Akhenaten's religious reforms. Nakht had shown the whole, rotting edifice that the King meant business. And despite being threatened with the wrath of Amun-Re, by his first priest, the young man was still alive. Akhenaten was also pleased with the news. He now knew that he had people that he could trust, who were not afraid of the old priesthood. His reforms and sequestrations could proceed at an even faster pace.

But there was one person who was less than pleased with Nakht – Nefertiti. Since the move to Armana, the two lovers had found it difficult to spend time alone. Some two days after his return to Armana they managed to snatch an hour together. Rather than making love, she passed the time berating him for murdering an old man. Nakht tried to explain his motives and the threats that the first priest had delivered. However, Nefertiti would have none of it. She accused him of becoming a cold blooded killer, acting on the instructions of her father and husband. For his own part, Nakht could see that she had a point. Although in his opinion, the priesthood needed to learn the lesson that he had taught it. But Nefertiti would not or could not see his point of view. Relations between them were distinctly cool.

Chapter Twelve

Nakht awoke in the middle of the night on the transport's foredeck. The blanket was soaking wet – but from the Admiral's red wine not his own sweat. He had nodded off before finishing the pitcher, which had been balanced on his chest. In his sleep he had overturned it, wetting both the sheet and his body with the red liquid. This wasn't the first time that such an accident had happened and he doubted that it would be the last. And looking on the bright side, it was preferable to pissing himself. That was something else that happened from time to time, when he was deeply under the influence. Feeling cold, he went to his sheltered berth and tried to accommodate his large frame in the small hammock. After several unsuccessful attempts, he lay on his side and curled himself up into a foetal position. It was less uncomfortable than his other efforts. Before the inevitable leg cramps set in *Nakht asked himself the question that had dominated his life...*

...Why had Nefertiti ended their affair? Nakht had initially put it down to his slaying of the High Priest at Karnak. Following their first awkward meeting, after his return to Armana, he had not been able to see her alone. Over a week passed without any further form of intimate communication from her. Finally, she had called him to one side and informed him that Akhenaten had business in Memphis. This would take both the Pharaoh and Ay away from Armana for up to a week. On the morning of their departure he was to report to her bedchamber. She had something to tell him. Nakht could see from her expression that it was unlikely to be something that he wanted to hear. He had to wait a further three days before his patron and the King sailed together downstream. Although Ay was still officially the

master of the King's horses, his influence had kept growing, following the death of Ramose. This was partly because Akhenaten had very little time for affairs of state. His main interest was the new religion and his battles against the priesthoods. But as far as Egypt's politics, economics and foreign affairs were concerned, he preferred to leave such matters to others. And Ay was only too willing to deputise for his master in this respect.

After they had departed for Memphis, Nakht approached the Queen's bedchamber with a feeling of great foreboding unsettling his stomach. Nefertiti was waiting for him alone, having dismissed her attendants. As he entered the room he saw that she was sat on the edge of the bed, fully clothed. She also had a pensive expression on her face. Turning to face him, she said without any form of greeting, "I have spoken to my father Ay. We both think that it is best for you to return back into his service. So when he returns from Memphis you will be working for him full time. Now you may return to your duties..."

As her voice tailed off, Nefertiti looked away and avoided making any eye contact with him. Nakht had been brought up to respect his betters, especially during his nine years of service with Ay. But after the intimacy and closeness that he had experienced with Nefertiti, he was not prepared to be dismissed in such a haughty manner. Instead of leaving he asked, "Why are you talking to me like this? Is it because I topped that old priest at Karnak or is it..."

"You have already been told to go!" the Queen interrupted angrily, "Please, stop trying my patience and follow my instructions!" Nakht took a half step towards her and then thought better of it. If this was how Nefertiti wanted to end things between them, then he had no real choice. He bowed and said, "Forgive me,

Queen Nefer-Nefru-Aten, I forgot myself for a moment. It will not happen again." But as he turned to walk out of the room, he could see from her face that his use of her new given name had struck home. It was precisely the effect that he had desired it to have.

For the next seven days he tried to think of the reasons behind her words. He doubted that it was the killing of the priest – alone. Nefertiti usually had as much time for the priesthood as her father and husband. Maybe the danger posed by their illicit affair had become too much for her to handle. They obviously had not yet been discovered in their infidelity by the Pharaoh. If that was the case, then the both of them would be dead already. And then another possibility came to him. Had she been reconciled with her husband? It seemed to come back down to the time he had spent removing the engravings. While he had been safeguarding gangs of workmen erasing carvings in Karnak, the direct opposite had been taking place in Armana. Inside the newly built temple of the Aten craftsmen had been at work creating new images. Originally these had shown Akhenaten with his hands raised towards the solar disc, accepting the bounty of the Aten's rays. But recently, new images had started to appear. The first of these had shown the King and Queen sat together on the same level, on either side of the sun disc. The second showed them stood together, with two of their daughters, absorbing the Aten's radiance. Nakht found this aspect of the new religion confusing. Initially, Akhenaten had stated that he was the only person capable of approaching the Aten. But now it seemed as if Nefertiti had been given the same powers. Whatever the religious significance of the carvings, they seemed to signify that the Queen had been raised to a level almost equal to her husband. And to his mind, that could only signify a rapprochement between the two.

Against that, he thought about the expression on her face when he had left the Queen's bedchamber. His use of her new name had struck some sort of raw nerve. Possibly she was not yet a fully paid up member of the new creed. Or it could be, that she still retained some feelings for him and did not like his use of her official name? But it wasn't until Ay returned from Memphis that he was given another reason. The Vizier in waiting was in a good mood following his trip with Akhenaten. Shortly after his arrival in Armana, he summoned Nakht to his private apartments. These were located in the heart of Akhenaten's palace, but sufficiently secluded to be out of earshot. Ay had left his wife Tiy and his butler Hor in Thebes. Ostensibly, this was to take care of the family home. Although Nakht knew that it was really to get away from them. When he walked into the main room Ay was sat in front of a mirror, at his dressing table. He was putting on the finishing touches to his make up. When his lips were sufficiently reddened he said, "And how is my poor bear with a sore head?"

There was nothing effeminate about men wearing make up in Egypt. For one thing it acted as a sunscreen. Nakht chose not to wear it, because his dark skin protected him against the sun. But Ay was very rarely in the sun. His use of make up appeared to be purely cosmetic, as the older man liked to appear many years younger than he actually was. But before Nakht could reply, Ay resumed, "I take it that the Queen has spoken to you. She told me that she would. So listen to me and pay heed to what I say. You were both taking a chance. Now that Akhenaten has her at his side in Armana, your time for fun and games is over. She has to be the dutiful wife and priestess. But it is not quite as simple as that, I'm sorry to say." Nakht was confused, so remained silent as Ay was obviously note done yet.

"She's pregnant you fool! And there's every chance that it's yours."
Still keeping quiet, Nakht thought about the last time that he had made love to Nefertiti. It had been about a month before his visit to the temple at Karnak. They had been rather careless over recent times, with Nefertiti allowing him to shoot inside her. Ay watched his brow reflect these thoughts and continued,
"So now she has to...er...how shall I put it? Cuddle up to her husband and hope that his religious zeal will distract him from the problems caused by an eight month pregnancy!"

As he finally finished, the older man placed his wig on his head and adjusted it in the mirror. Nakht was still lost for words. His own potential danger did not unduly concern him. But he found the incongruity of the situation bizarre. The Pharaoh's father in law had just informed him that his married daughter was carrying Nakht's child. Obviously. it would have been better to hear the news first hand from Nefertiti. And hopefully her "cuddling up", as Ay had put it, would be successful enough to remove her from danger.
Ay let him consider these issues for a few moments, until he was satisfied that his wig was correctly aligned. Then he swivelled around to face Nakht and said, "Now you must put this behind you. I do hope that you didn't make the mistake of falling in love with her?"

Again, Nakht made no reply. Ay swallowed and raised his eyebrows saying, "I can tell your answer by the way that you are staring at your sandals. Never mind, my boy, it's all in the past now. She does have a sister you know, although she's not quite as beautiful..."

"Do you mean Mutnodjme?" Nakht interjected, thinking that in his eyes, she was no substitute for Nefertiti. Even though the sister was an attractive woman and her very name meant sweet mother. It was not something that appealed to him after his liaison with Nefertiti.

"Yes...er...but perhaps not," Ay responded, "Now that I've mentioned her, I seem to remember promising her hand to Horemheb, when we were in Memphis. He's getting quite ambitious despite his relative youth. But marrying into the family of the Vizier and Chancellor of Armana should calm him down a bit."

That last statement snapped Nakht out of his self pity and he asked, "So Akhenaten has promoted you to be his Vizier?"

Ay smiled and answered,"Of course. I knew it would only be a matter of time. And your endeavours with Nefertiti helped me a great deal. If my dear daughter had ever required any convincing of the need to advance my cause with her husband. But no, I shall say no more. Instead we shall celebrate together this evening. My investiture is in two days' time."

Not for the first or last time in Ay's service, Nakht felt as if he had been used. But rather than ranting or raving he accepted his patron's words calmly and said, "You have my congratulations for your success. But what do you have in mind for me, now that I am no longer to command the Queen's personal guard?"

Ay hesitated, for just a moment, before replying, "I have decided to form my own personal guard. Horemheb will shortly be moving to Armana, where he will take charge of the King's guard. That means that I need a counter balance to his influence with the army. I also need a body of men around me that can be relied upon. They must be able to go out into Egypt to enforce the Pharaoh's decrees. There are many minor temples that still need to be closed down. Their priests require strict discipline and their assets must be sequestered. Can you do this for me...and er, the King, of course?"

Other than returning to Bathar, Nakht had little option. So he said, "I have done your bidding to the exact letter for ten years. And I will continue to do it, for as long as you need me."

Ay nodded at this reply and went onto say, "Good. Now I will say only one thing further. When you were fourteen and waiting to meet the Pharaoh for the first time we had words. I told you that we could go a long way together. That is still the case. Although I am now officially the Vizier, or will be in two days time, that is not the end of our journey. Bear those words in mind, Nakht!"

No reply was needed and none was given. Instead the two men made arrangements to meet that night and celebrate Ay's promotion. Nakht left his patron's apartments in a confused mood. The older man had obviously brought him together with Nefertiti to further his career. He had accomplished his aims, so now their affair was over. Nakht had been promoted, which was no bad thing. But at twenty two years of age he was beginning to feel more than a little dissatisfied. He had no home or land. There was no mate in his life and other than the King's Gold of Honour, he had no personal wealth. All he had was a vague promise of personal advancement when Ay fulfilled his goals. For the moment that was enough to keep him going. But it was not until five years later that he discovered the real reason why Nefertiti had ended their affair. Under Ay's influence and despite her unwanted pregnancy, she had decided to become a man...

Chapter Thirteen

As the sun rose over the Nile, Djar found his commanding officer precariously balanced; part in and part out of his hammock. He saw that Nakht seemed to be sleeping peacefully and was initially reluctant to wake him. The junior soldier was well aware of the agonies that his superior went through every night. They had served together for over five years in the border struggles against the Hittites in Syria. So in that time, he had got used to the taciturn Commander and his ways. Because he had only Nakht's legend and his own experience to rely upon, Djar knew that he was only aware of a small part of the man's whole story. During his five years of service he had realised that his Commander was tormented by dark and evil demons. How this had come to pass Djar could only guess at. He lacked the courage or will to ask Nakht face to face about his troubles. Besides such a question was inappropriate from a younger and much junior subordinate. Putting his reluctance to wake Nakht to one side, he grasped his arm and said, "Commander, the sun has risen. Please wake up...I have some bad news from the Admiral..."

Nakht snapped out of his sleep and opened his eyes to see Djar standing over him. As the second in command repeated his words Nakht replied, "So what is this bad news? It has to be more palatable than our breakfast will be, so spit it out, man!"

Djar was slightly wrong footed by his superior's attempt at humour. But he recovered sufficiently to say, "There is no wind, sir. In the Admiral's opinion we will be becalmed until the afternoon at least!"

Nakht had a broad smile on his face, as he hauled himself out of the hammock and said, "You call that bad news. Nonsense! Organise the men. At last we can do some rowing and get our bodies back into some sort of shape."

"But what about Lord Ay and his wedding gift? We are going to lose time..."

"Very little time, if we put our backs into it!" As the walked into the open air, Nakht licked and raised his forefinger towards the north. Admiral Habt was quite right. Not only was there no breeze from the north, and apart from that which was inside his buttocks, there appeared to be no prospect of wind from anywhere. He grinned at Djar before saying, ""If Lord Ay was here then I would gladly offer him this finger to sit upon. Now, go and get the men ready for some hard work. They have been sitting on their arses and getting fat for the last three days."

The boat had fifteen oars on each side. Of these twelve were located on the two bows. On the stern there were three on each to the port and starboard sides. Although the Admiral had sufficient sailors to man half the oars, Nakht was insistent that his men took the majority of the positions. Admiral Habt put this down to the Commander's desire to reach Thebes in good time. But he was wrong. Nakht wanted to row against the current, like he had done many times before. He descended into the bow and took the first oar, on the river side. When the sailors had finished their job of releasing the moorings he shouted, "Pull in time with me. If any man from the navy or the army, causes a loss of rhythm he will answer to me. Is that understood by everybody?"

There was an all round unenthusiastic response of "Yes, sir!". Then slowly, as the men struggled to co-ordinate their strokes, the transport set off.
One of the reasons why Nakht enjoyed rowing so much, was that once the crew had settled into a rhythm, it all

became automatic. Pull, lift, feather, dip and then pull again. Provided it was done in unison, they would lose almost no time in reaching Thebes. Ay's wedding could not be delayed. At least the man was not preparing to marry his own daughter, like Akhenaten had done, more than once. *Lord Ay was only engaged to marry his own grand daughter...*

...In the years following Ay's promotion to Vizier, Nakht had been kept very busy. In both upper and lower Egypt there were many temples of the old religion. Just as he had done in Thebes, Nakht took soldiers and masons to the religious buildings on behalf of the King. They had erased prominent engravings and confiscated what assets they could. These were all taken back to Armana, where they were badly needed. Especially the gold, which Akhenaten personally distributed to the obsequious populace of his new city, as if it was stale bread. Nakht rarely spent more than a few weeks at a time in Armana. During most of the next five years he travelled the length and breadth of the country. In that time, while he was carrying out his duties, he hadn't actually killed anybody. He had given several protesters quite severe beatings, especially if they had threatened the safety of his soldiers or workers. Usually the priests kept well out of his way, being aware of what had happened to the High Priest in Karnak. Once Nakht's name was mentioned they put great distance between themselves and their shrines. Then after a temple had been defaced and looted of what had not been hidden, he would return to Armana. There he would hand over the proceeds of each mission to Ay.

Nakht's duties were not only confined to confiscating the assets of temples. Due to the great resentment throughout Egypt, people were now unwilling to pay their taxes. When he was a child in Bathar the visit of the Pharaoh's officials had never been welcome. Although after each harvest, the villagers always handed the officials a large proportion of their crops without any dissent. It was regarded as a debt that was due to the King, for his tireless work in averting chaos. This tax was not something that his father had enjoyed paying, after all the family's hard work in the fields. Yet he looked upon it as something that was owed and recognised that it had to be paid. But since Akhenaten had proscribed all other gods, the farmers' attitude of respectful submission had evaporated. When Nakht was not ensuring the safety of his stone masons, he was supervising the officials who were collecting taxes.

In between times he returned to Armana, which was a totally different place to the rest of Egypt. He was there for the birth of Nefertiti's sixth daughter, which Nakht believed to be his own. She was called Neferneferure and Ay told him that the baby had his broad facial features, rather than the Pharaoh's unusually elongated face. Akhenaten had readily accepted that the baby had been born prematurely. Although he had also confided to the Vizier that he was upset that his great wife had not finally presented him with a son. But, apparently, the will of the solar god was paramount. If the Aten had decided that he should have another daughter, then so be it. As always Ay bowed to the King's perception and expressed the view that he wished that he had one tenth of Akhenaten's immense wisdom. The Pharaoh had taken his response in good part and offered him a personal blessing, by way of compensation for his deficiencies.

On these visits to Armana Nakht saw very little of Nefertiti and nothing of the child Neferneferure. In his new position, he had no reason to approach either and Nefertiti had no excuse to approach or contact him. When he did see her at court, her eyes now avoided his at all times. She studiously ignored him, preferring the company of her superintendent Meri-Re II. So he stood respectfully at Ay's shoulder and wondered if Neferneferure was really his daughter. Since Ay had forbidden him to take a wife he had often wondered what it would be like to be a father a child. And now that he possibly had, Nakht still found himself in the awkward position of wondering. In many ways he was glad to be out of Armana and in the countryside. It brought him back down to earth and reminded him about the real state of affairs in Egypt. Outside of Akhenaten's new capital, it appeared that nobody worshipped the Aten. Nakht was meeting with more and more resistance as he went about his duties. These were often carried out in conjunction with local police and officials. But no matter how quickly and efficiently he closed a temple down, the moment that his back was turned, its priesthood returned.

But in Armana the Pharaoh's reign was reaching its highest point. The magnificence of the Aten's temple and King's palace was beyond compare. Art and literature flourished, freed from the shackles of the old religion. Busts of Nefertiti were carved which were so lifelike, their owners would swear that she was present in the room. Akhenaten himself had written a stunning poem called "Hymn to the Sun". It was an eloquent and beautiful piece of writing. Ay had assured Nakht that the Pharaoh had composed it alone and without any sort of help. Magnificent tombs were also being constructed in the northern and southern cliff face. Ay had been one of the first in Armana to start work on his last resting place. He was over fifty years of age, much older than the Pharaoh. So it was a sensible act on his part to start his arrangements before it was too late. Although Nakht knew that the old sod had no intention of taking up residence in his own tomb, for a great many more years to come.

Life in Armana was also marked by elaborate festivals organised by the King. Akhenaten had established a willing priesthood of the Aten. This was headed by the High Priest, Meri-Re I and the chief servitor, Panhesy. Celebrations were held on a weekly basis. These were more to do with the worship of Akhenaten than the solar disc and they all revolved around the Pharaoh. After they were concluded the Pharaoh would distribute the gold, which had been looted from the temples and reworked, to his grateful subjects. And if there were no celebrations, the King would celebrate his divinity by riding his golden chariot around Armana. Following a strict east to west course, he would imitate the progress of the solar disc. To Nakht, who experienced both sides of life in Egypt, it all seemed very contrived and unreal. But dissent was not limited to the people of Egypt who lived outside of Armana. Rumbles of discontent were also coming from abroad.

Amenhotep III had been a consummate diplomat. He had founded Egypt's wealth on the benefits of peace and international trade. The world wanted wheat, wines and gold. Egypt had plentiful supplies of all three. She even had wood now that the Lebanon and parts of Syria were under her control. So the late Pharaoh had exported surplus goods and produce throughout the Mediterranean region. He had instigated and maintained good relations throughout the known world. Unfortunately his son, Akhenaten, was far too busy with organising the new religion to bother himself with such trivial matters. These were devolved in the first instance to Ay, but also increasingly to Horemheb. The latter's continued rise in the royal household went from strength to strength and he was soon promoted to the rank of general. But neither man had the power or authority to conclude a series of international negotiations. That could only be done by the King. And he was loath to let such mundane affairs get in the way of his new religion.

Matters came to a head when Ay had insisted that he granted the foreign diplomats, now based at Armana, an audience. Protocol, which demanded regular weekly meetings, had been ignored for too long. The Vizier had been made aware of the dignitaries dissatisfaction, in no uncertain terms. So he had used all his influence on the King to insist that the foreign ambassadors were to be received. Akhenaten had agreed reluctantly, but promised to listen to their concerns. Ay was worried because the Pharaoh may have been grudging in his assent, but he had granted it far too easily. On the day of the audience these fears were more than justified. The diplomats arrived at the appointed hour and entered the palace courtyard. It was one hour before noon and the heat was starting to get quite unbearable. The courtyard was an open but enclosed space. Initially the dignitaries had no concerns, especially as Ay was there to greet them. But when they saw the expression on his face their attitude changed. With great regret, the Vizier informed them that the King was not ready to receive them. He had been detained by important internal matters of state, but would summon them shortly. They watched in annoyance as Ay scurried back into the cool confines of the palace building.

The foreign emissaries were now between a rock and a hard place. They had requested the meeting and the Pharaoh had granted it. So they had turned up wearing their official robes of office. These were quite heavy and not what any person would want to wear in the midday sun. Leaving the palace courtyard was out of the question. Protocol demanded that after setting foot inside the royal residence, they had to remain until dismissed by the ruler. And until Akhenaten had received them, they could not be dismissed. Refreshments were also a problem. Protocol also demanded that as guests they were unable to ask for water or food. Hospitality could be accepted, but first it had to be offered. Akhenaten was in no mood to offer either water or shade from the heat. The diplomats were kept standing in the sun for three hours and Ay was nowhere to be seen.

Not all of the ambassadors were on their feet for the full three hours. Several reached the point of dehydration and collapsed in the courtyard. But the leader of the Hittite's delegation was made of sterner stuff. As colleagues from other countries and even his own subordinates keeled over, he stood his corner. Every so often he would glance up at the palace building. And from one of the small front windows, on the upper floors, he sometimes glimpsed a grinning, elongated face. The subsequent audience was short and achieved little. Conversely, the diplomats' reports to their rulers were long and achieved a great deal. Outside of Egypt it became common knowledge in most courts, that the Pharaoh was a malevolent and deformed madman.

Nakht had been away from Armana during this episode. But when he returned to the city a month later, Ay was still furious. All the credibility, which he had worked so hard to achieve, with the foreign ambassadors was gone. On the other hand, Nakht had to stifle a little smile. It wasn't often that the Vizier came unstuck in such a dramatic way. Perhaps Akhenaten was cleverer than the soldier had thought him to be. Although his patron would not be placated. As the younger man left his chambers, the Vizier's final words ran through his mind. Ay had said quite calmly but forcefully, "We shall put a stop to this nonsense and we will do it soon. I am not prepared to tolerate internal dissent in my country and external contempt beyond it, for much longer!"

Chapter Fourteen

At lunch on the third day of the journey up the Nile, even the Admiral noticed that Nakht's mood had improved. It seemed as if the morning's rowing had done him a power of good. The powerfully built Commander sat with his men and the crew and ate a good sized plate of food. This was washed down with several cups of beer. For once the sweat that flowed from Nakht's body was not induced by alcohol, but by his earlier labours. He didn't go quite so far as laughing and joining in the men's General conversations. But his attitude and body language spoke for him. Although this relaxed mood did not last. Just before the meal concluded the wind picked up. Admiral Habt ordered his crew to unfurl the sails and dismissed the men assigned to the afternoon's rowing detail. Nakht frowned at this change of weather and returned to his berth. They were now just over a day away from Thebes. Provided the vessel maintained its pace and course, Lord Ay would have his wedding present before the following day's sunset. *And then a lifetime of scheming, planning and plotting would achieve its ultimate goal...*

...Following the incident with the foreign emissaries, Ay had tried to take a firmer line with the Pharaoh. But it was like trying to spin linen from sand. What you ended up with, was exactly what you had started out with. Provided that Akhenaten believed the worship of the Aten was being properly observed, the King had no other political interests. Beyond the confines of Armana this was only achieved by increased brutality. Even inside the city many of the people who gratefully accepted their ruler's golden benevolence, made offerings to Amun-re in the privacy of their homes. Outside of the country, the Hittites sensed a leader who

had completely lost the plot. There were repeated incursions into the northern part of Egypt's empire. But it was the state of Egypt's economy that was causing Ay the most worry.

To begin with, building a new city in the desert had placed enormous strain on the nation's finances and infrastructure. Workers' enforced levies had been removed from building and maintaining Egypt's roads and irrigation channels to construct Armana. On top of that, the new priesthood and religion needed to be funded. Gold was still relatively plentiful, as the mines in Nubia and Wadi Hammamat were worked to their optimum levels of production. But the other main source of gold had dried up. After five years of looting and sequestration the old temples' assets had now been exhausted. Even the minor temples in the delta had been cleaned out. But as soon as the remaining supplies of the precious metal came into Armana, the King gave it away. International trade, the life blood of the New Kingdom, was also in decline. And all because the Pharaoh could not be bothered to sign renewal treaties with the trading partners that his late father had courted so assiduously.

Although the Pharaoh's introspection could not be entirely ascribed to his religious mania. Nor could it be blamed on his cloistered existence in Armana. Akhenaten reached the high point of his reign in its twelfth year. The thirteenth year became the start of his decline. And the start of his rule's slide into oblivion did not come from internal or foreign dissent. It came from a series of personal tragedies and disagreements. Rather surprisingly Ay took no part in the tragedies, but he was heavily involved in the disagreements. Nefertiti was also involved – because of her quest to become a man. Nakht was involved in neither. He spent most of the next three years in Syria with Horemheb, patrolling

Egypt's northern border. Although the King had no stomach for military affairs, Ay and Horemheb decided to reinforce the military presence on the northern boundary. They had concluded that unless some form of action was taken, then the Hittites would feel free to march south. And then Egypt would face a rerun of the earlier Hyksos invasions. In Syria, Nakht was involved in a series of skirmishes with the Hittites. Although they were not fully blown battles, they enhanced his reputation as a strong soldier and a competent Commander.

But back in Armana, Akhenaten was about to enter his own personal underworld. The first incident in the ruler's decline started with the plague that swept Egypt in the thirteenth and fourteenth years of his reign. Neferneferure, the youngest of the King's daughters, and the one that Nakht believed that he had fathered, succumbed to the plague and died. He was away on active service when this happened and was given the news by Horemheb. Nakht was unaware as to the extent of the general's knowledge about his affair with Nefertiti. But as Ay's son-in-law and confidant, the Commander assumed that the Horemheb knew the full story. Despite Nakht's increasing misanthropy and detachment from his fellow beings, he mourned the loss of the young daughter that he had never known.

Before he was able to return to Armana, further sad news reached the frontier region. The royal couple's next youngest daughter, Setepenre also fell victim to the plague and died. This was reported by the same messenger that brought Nakht his orders to return to Armana. Lord Ay had need of his services and wished him to resume charge of his personal guard. Although the presence of Horemheb's forces had caused the Hittites to temper their territorial ambitions, Nakht knew that their threat was still present. So for Ay to recall him at this time could only mean that the Vizier was planning his next move. And whatever that was, it meant trouble for somebody. In his wildest dreams, Nakht never imagined that the somebody was Akhenaten.

The Commander was almost thirty by the time that he returned to Armana at Ay's bidding. Akhenaten's capital city looked as prosperous to him as it had two years earlier, before his departure to Syria. But the intervening two years spent away from Armana had honed his instincts. Life in the border region was real. There was no show or pretence out there. One mistake could lead to a Hittite sword or arrow in the back. So as he walked through the city towards the palace, he knew that he was walking through a dream. Almost everybody that he saw looked wealthy. They were wearing fine linen and golden jewellery. But in the streets there were fewer people and more litter around than he remembered. No doubt that was down to the plague. Although he did think to himself that the plague, which had now passed, could not account for the people's expressions. Initially Nakht could not place these strange looks. But finally it dawned upon him. The citizens of Armana had the same demeanour of the tomb robbers that he witnessed in the palace of Malkarta, fifteen years earlier. They also knew that their end was in sight and that it wasn't going to be particularly pleasant.

Inside the palace he was ushered to Ay's chambers by attendants that he did not recognise. Ay, of course, he did recognise. In his wig and make up, the old fraud did not look a day older than he did the last time that Nakht had seen him. But a quick bout of mental arithmetic told the younger man that Ay was fast approaching fifty eight years of age. And the make up did seem to be applied a little more heavily, than he remembered it to have been. Although to his credit, the

Vizier seemed genuinely pleased to see Nakht. He walked over to him and said, "It is good to have you back here. I have missed you these two years, my little marsh boy!"

Nakht was surprised at the warmth of his greeting and replied, "Honestly...you are speaking the truth?"

"Of course I am," Ay responded, with a hurt look on his face, "I have only two people in this world that I can trust. Your are one and my old friend and son-in-law Horemheb is the other. For two long years you have both been away from me. Admittedly, you were carrying out duties of national importance, but that did not lessen my feeling of loss in any way!"

Such an overt show of sincerity sounded bad. To Nakht's ears it could only mean that there was killing to be done. Rather than reply he let Ay continue, "But to business. You return to Armana at a most interesting time. If I were to say that there are plenty of opportunities for men like ourselves, would you know what I mean?"

Nakht thought carefully for a moment before saying, "Only if you tell me. Remember, I have been out in the field for some time."

"How can I ever forget that? I had many good reports from Horemheb about your work in Syria. He told me that you had personally killed between twenty and thirty Hittites in the course of your duties. And that you always brought every member of your patrol back to the barracks!"

"I lost count of the bodies, after slaying the first ten northerners. But there was and is still much more work to be done."

Ay did not reply immediately. The Vizier paced the room, as if he was trying to get his thoughts together. The younger man could plainly see that he was very agitated. Eventually the senior courtier said, "You did well in Syria. If it meant anything these days, you would get the King's Gold of Honour again. But listen, about my problems. Everything is about to blow up and I can't keep the lid on the pot for any longer. Although the gods themselves know that I have tried."

Nakht smiled at his discomfort and asked, "Which pot is overheating and beyond your control Lord Ay?"

"You can start by taking that smug grin off your face – otherwise I won't say another word. Then you can tell me what is wrong with these bloody Pharaohs. Why do they all want to fuck their own daughters! Isn't screwing their sisters and minor wives enough for them?"

Having forced out the words, Ay sighed heavily and summoned a servant. He instructed the man to bring them a large jug of wine. Then he led Nakht into his innermost office. After pouring two large cups of wine he said,
"You know that the plague claimed two of the princesses, including your child. Well now Akhenaten believes that his bloodline is in peril. So he's started on his remaining daughters. He married Mekytaten six months ago and she is about to give birth. The baby is due any day, it could even be born tomorrow. He's also knocking off Merytaten and Ankhesenpaaten. According to the Pharaoh, the crown prince Tutankhaten is such a sickly child that he could pop off at any moment. He wants another son."

As Ay paused to take a sip of his wine Nakht asked, "It is like you said earlier, our rulers are renowned for such things. So where's the problem?"

"With my oldest daughter, Nefertiti. She took the deaths of her two daughters very hard. Not to put to fine a point on things, she doesn't want her husband passing his deformities on through his other daughters. They're too close to him for any children to be normal.

So she has decided to retire from royal life. She gave Akhenaten an ultimatum. Our daughters or me. There was no competition. They're in his bed every night and he's preparing her funerary statues..."

"What do you mean...is he going to kill her?" Nakht interrupted.

"Oh, no – but only out of respect for me. Instead we all have to pretend that she's dead. You know, stricken from the record, that sort of thing. She's going to retire from public life and go and live in Memphis. I don't know what will happen to me...that's why I need somebody that I can trust at my side."

Knowing the Vizier as he did, Nakht was not entirely convinced that he was getting the whole truth. But he recognised the look of fear on his patron's face. Could this have been one of his schemes that had gone badly astray?

Within a week events took a turn for the worse. Mekytaten died while giving birth to her father's child and the baby was stillborn. When this happened Nefertiti was true to her word and departed for Memphis. Although Nakht still had deep feelings for her, his respect for the former Queen vanished at this act. She had saved her own life by getting out of Armana. But that still left the freakish Pharaoh to force himself on Merytaten and Ankhesenpaaten. In one way he was glad that the daughter had never known, had been taken by the plague. That had to be a better fate than being raped by her acknowledged father. And even though Nefertiti had left Armana, he had still had a strange feeling that Ay was holding something back from him. Nakht had no doubt that he would eventually find out out what it was. That was once the Vizier decided that it was time for him to know. Initially though, his services were not required. Ay seemed to regain his composure now that Nakht was at his side. And the

Pharaoh showed no sign of wanting to replace his most senior and trusted official.

Chapter Fifteen

An afternoon of enforced idleness had caused Nakht to retreat into his shell again. The evening of the third night on the transport found him attacking the red wine and nibbling at his food. Not even Djar attempted to engage him in conversation. He could see that his superior officer had returned to one of his dark, introspective moods. Admiral Habt was relieved that there was less than twenty four hours before his mission ended. The sooner he could get Nakht off his ship the better. It wasn't just the man's surly attitude that annoyed him, but the fact that he was drinking his personal stock of red wine, as if it was water or beer. In his opinion, the soldiers' Commander was a complete alcoholic and not somebody that Habt personally considered as officer class. If the man didn't have the patronage of Lord Ay, then the Admiral would not have given him the time of day. But given the strength of his connections and his known propensity for violence, he bade the soldier a good night. Then he told his orderlies to ensure that they regularly topped up the Commander's jug of wine.

Nakht gratefully accepted the orderlies' offer, before he retired to the foredeck with his blanket. He gazed up at the night sky for a while. Then he thought to himself that *at least this time he was not returning to Ay too soon...*

...His early recall from Syria to Armana had been a complete waste of his time. Ay had been worried for his safety because of Nefertiti's abdication of her position as the King's great wife. But with his two young daughters to sleep with, Akhenaten had not missed his wife. There had been no threat to Ay's life or his position as Vizier. The King didn't even bat any eyelid when Kiya, the most

important of his minor wives, decided to return to the Hittites. The Pharaoh had married her as part of a peace treaty that had been agreed with the northern warriors many years ago. She had borne him his only son, Tutankhaten, the crown prince. But since the resumption of hostilities between the two nations, like Nefertiti before her, she had decided to leave Armana. Akhenaten who was consumed by both his religion and the lust for his daughters, gave her permission to depart. Her son, the heir apparent, was to remain in Armana. But the northern princess was allowed to go back to her people. It fell to Nakht to escort Kiya to the ever changing northern border and return her to Egypt's enemies. Then he went back into service with Horemheb, for almost two years, before he received Ay's next summons.

When he returned to Armana he saw even fewer people around than there had been before. And almost all the side streets were full, not just with litter but debris and excrement. As Akhenaten had stopped visiting the areas where ordinary people lived, the Pharaoh missed this vital sign. His subjects were deserting his new city in droves. But the King was more concerned with Ankhesenpaaten's pregnancy, than his crumbling regime. If anything, the situation in Egypt had deteriorated even further in the two years following Nakht's initial recall to Armana. The problems did not just come from abroad. Horemheb skilfully kept the northern menace in check. To the south, Nubia was so integrated and subjugated that its soldiers provided the Egyptian army with some of its best warriors. So it was internally, that the threat to stability had arisen. As Ay put it to Nakht, the power of the state had almost ceased to exist. No matter how many soldiers and police officers were sent out to the districts they encountered dissent. Quite often this was violent and not easily put down. Even Mahu, the chief of police in Armana, had his hands full. Public dissent, tax evasion and petty crime were now starting to spiral out of control in Akhenaten's very heartland.

It was time for a change. In the seventeenth year of the King's reign Ay realised that serious action had to be taken. Otherwise, the country could easily tumble head first into civil war. And as the most senior person in the new Kingdom, apart from the Pharaoh, it was his job to appraise Akhenaten of the facts. It took several weeks for a meeting to be granted, due to the King's never ending religious duties. Ay had also taken the precaution of recalling Horemheb from Syria. The two soldiers and the Vizier had discussed their strategy well in advance of their audience with Akhenaten. If the Pharaoh refused to accept Ay's ultimatum and compromise, the Vizier would take the throne. When the day of their audience finally arrived, they entered the throne room together. Only Nakht and Horemheb were armed. But apart from his four fan bearers, the King only had Meri-Re I, the High Priest and the Aten's chief servitor, Panhesy, present. The Vizier had also ensured that the police chief, Mahu, had been sent on a fool's errand to the south of Armana. He had gone willingly and was fully aware of Ay's intentions, having also recognised that drastic action was required.

Akhenaten was wearing the religious Atef, or the white crown of the upper Kingdom. He also wore his Pharonic beard to emphasise his status. Ay approached the throne without prostrating himself, incurring the Pharaoh's immediate displeasure. Turning to Meri-Re I and then to Panhesy, Akhenaten said angrily, in his odd lisping tone, "Such disrespect should not go unpunished. The Aten will not be pleased! Don't you both agree?"

Neither the priest or the servitor replied, other than a half hearted mumble of assent. The gravity of their immediate situation was beginning to dawn upon them. Ignoring all three men, Ay immediately took centre stage and forcefully stated, "I am sorry to say, your majesty, that the will of the Aten is not even followed in your city of Armana these days. But although your reign is over, there may be a compromise that will save your life..."

"Compromise?" Akhenaten responded furiously, "You dare to offer me – a living god, compromise. It is in my mind to order the Aten to strike you all down now for your rank disloyalty and disobedience!"

Ay sighed heavily and replied in an exasperated tone, "Call on the Aten. And see what good it will do you. I came here to save your life. But if you are in no mood to listen to my words, then so be it. Nakht, please carry out your orders!"

Until now Nakht had never enjoyed rituals of attending court. But he did enjoy testing himself against the gods, whether he was threatened with the wrath of Amun or the Aten. He also knew that Ay had wasted his breath by speaking to Akhenaten. So when the Vizier issued his instructions, the Commander pushed past Ay and Horemheb. Then he walked over to the throne and drew his curved sword before saying, "Summon your precious Aten, freak. No priest or any other mortal man has ever succeeded in staying my sword arm. And they all called upon every god in creation before they died!"

Akhenaten was horrified. Burly, horrible looking subjects were not supposed to address a living god, let alone threaten him. The Pharaoh screamed, "Guards, I summon you. Mahu, come quickly, your King is in grave danger..."

There was no reply. As well as ensuring the police chief's absence, Horemheb had dismissed the King's guard, in its entirety, before the audience. Panhesy and Meri-Re I suddenly looked extremely worried and began to tremble. The fan bearers had dropped their fans and were huddled together in a corner of the room. Nakht turned to face Ay and shouted, "Are you really sure that you want me to go ahead? This madman will never accept any compromise. Besides there can be no turning back now that we have come this far!"

The Vizier glanced at Horemheb for reassurance. The General nodded his assent. Ay then said to Nakht, "Go ahead. Kill all three of them and do it quickly."

With one blow Nakht swung his sharpened scimitar into Panhesy's neck, severing the servitor's head from his body. Before Panhesy's torso had hit the floor, the Commander had plunged his sword into Meri-Re's stomach. It was a mortal wound and left the priest squealing loudly. Leaving the weapon inside the Aten's Chief Priest, he walked towards the Pharaoh. Akhenaten was shaking with fear as his hands grasped the throne tightly. He was speechless and unable to even call upon the Aten for assistance. But Nakht showed him no mercy. It had been agreed beforehand that the King should have no sign of any wounds or bruises. Using his immense strength, Nakht pulled Akhenaten up from the royal throne. He span the Pharaoh round so that the King's back was pressed against his own chest. Then he placed his large hand over Akhenaten's mouth and nose, pushing his head back, into the centre of his own chest. The ruler struggled, but could not escape Nakht's firm grip. Within three minutes he suffocated and the soldier let the Pharaoh's lifeless body fall to the floor of the throne room. There were no noticeable bruises or external wounds.

Ay looked at Akhenaten's corpse and said to Horemheb, "Well, I rather think this puts an end to the Armana experiment, don't you?"

The General initially looked less sure and not as relaxed as the Vizier. He was a younger man and seemed worried about being involved in the killing of a Pharaoh. Nakht on the other hand was more concerned about his sword. He pulled it from Meri-Re's stomach and started to clean it on the dead man's tunic. While he was doing this, Ay walked over to the vacant throne. Rather than assuming it, which both Nakht and Horemheb had expected he said,

"Gentlemen. May I present you both with our next ruler. Smenkhkare, I respectfully call upon you to enter the throne room and assume your royal office!"

The doors to the throne room opened and a slight figure, wearing a heavy cloak walked in. Nakht recognised something very familiar about the person, who was wearing the Nemes headdress and a Pharonic beard. At first the person's identity did dawn upon him. But just as Horemheb opened his mouth to speak, the Commander's mind clicked. He turned and shouted, "Smenkhkare, my arse. That's your daughter, Nefertiti, Ay!"

"No it isn't," the Vizier responded, his voice full of mock indignation, "It's our country's new Pharaoh. Let me remind you both, that Egypt has had a female ruler before. Hatshepsut's reign and her monuments were glorious. She even restored trade with the Kingdom of Punt. In our time of need, the nation needs her sort again..."

Nefertiti or Smenkhkare had already assumed the throne. Before sitting down, she threw off her cloak and interjected, "These things will work themselves out, as they usually do when a ruler has been deposed. Now, I suggest that you start making the arrangements for my former husband's burial. He can occupy his magnificent tomb – albeit some years before he expected to. Then we can all return to Memphis and get away from the shit storm that's about to burst all over this miserable, fucking place!"

She spoke with assurance and authority. It was as if she had been born to rule and the moment had finally arrived. Nefertiti sat on the throne, almost completely oblivious to the three dead bodies that were surrounding her. In killing Akhenaten, Nakht realised that yet again he had done Ay's bidding. And yet again the Vizier had wrong footed him. Nefertiti was to be the new Pharaoh and known as Smenkhkare. And to do so she had become a man, without a husband. But Ay was known for playing the long game. When Nefertiti had been disillusioned with her husband, Ay had pushed him towards her. They had become lovers – but only for as long as it it had suited Ay's purposes. He could now see know that Nefertiti's father had decided that she must become a man, so that she could take the throne of Egypt. Probably because the Vizier didn't want it for himself – yet!

At Nakht's side Horemheb stood quietly. If this twist to their scheme had surprised the General, he somehow managed to keep his feelings well concealed. The senior officer had recovered the composure that he had momentarily lost, following the death of Akhenaten. Turning to Ay, Horemheb said, "What shall we do about the royal fan bearers? We really should kill them as well, just to be on the safe side. The fewer witnesses there are the better, don't you think Ay?"

Following Vizier's nod of assent, the General drew his sword and gestured for Nakht to accompany him. Then he moved purposefully towards the weeping attendants and stabbed May, the former ruler's fan bearer to the right. The junior soldier followed him reluctantly. Nakht did not relish the prospect of killing all the fan bearers, but the job having been started needed to be completed.

Chapter Sixteen

At least Nakht didn't spill his pitcher of wine all over himself that night. Before nodding off, on the Nile transport's foredeck, he made sure that every last drop was finished. Then he put the the Admiral's clay jug to one side and curled up for his night's sleep. To his surprise, Nakht found himself slipping into unconsciousness very easily. It had to be down to his morning's effort on the oars, he told himself. Perhaps it would be better if he left the army and joined Egypt's navy. That way he might get a decent night's sleep more often. Although he slept well, by his own standards, it was still dark when he awoke. And he was sweating heavily. Rather than seek out his hammock, he decided to persevere with the stretching out on the foredeck. After wrapping the blanket tightly around his body, his mind wandered back *to the aftermath of Akhenaten's death in Armana...*

...Where the three regicides escaped the potentially fatal consequences of their actions. Across Egypt, the news of the heretic's death was greeted with celebrations which had not been matched since the Hyksos were defeated. But Ay still had a lot of tidying up work to do in the aftermath. To begin with he issued a proclamation which stated that the King had died of natural causes. Due to Nakht's skilful work, there were no external bruises or abrasions on Akhenaten's body. His testament was confirmed by the embalmers, shortly after they started their seventy day task. Nobody sought to question the disappearance of the two leading members of the Aten's priesthood. It was assumed that they had fled from Armana in the aftermath of the King's demise. And only the families of the four fan bearers asked about their menfolk's absence. Their lone voices

were ignored. They were drowned out by the spontaneous clamour of joy that erupted across the country.

Even the news of Nefertiti's accession to the throne, as Smenkhkare, was well received. Ay's instructions to his officials described her as a prince of the royal household. Nefertiti's legitimacy was soon to be established and reinforced by her marriage into the royal bloodline. This was strangely true because after much persuading by her grandfather, the King's daughter Merytaten, agreed to "marry" her own mother. The marriage cemented the new Pharaoh's rule in the eyes of the Egyptian people. Although Nakht found the arrangement slightly odd, he thought that it might be a relief to the child. At least she no longer had her father's sexual advances to contend with. The Vizier presided over the private marriage and coronation ceremonies at Armana. There were few people permitted to be present to witness either. Since the death of Akhenaten, the remaining inhabitants had been fleeing the city in even greater numbers. Armana, which had been a meal ticket to so many, had been transformed into a poisoned chalice. Both Ay and Smenkhkare were well aware of the backlash that awaited the late Pharaoh's city in the desert.

Which was why, three months after Akhenaten's death and his subsequent entombment, the royal family left for Memphis. In her quasi retirement from public life, Nefertiti had set up home there. Although Ay had initially wanted to return to Thebes, which was the epicentre of the New Kingdom's power. But he realised that it was too soon to do so. Some healing time needed to pass before that aim could be achieved. There were few better places to spend such time than in Memphis. For a start it was known as the old secular capital of Egypt, which dated back to the old Kingdom.

The move to Memphis sent out the correct signals to the majority of the populace. Along with Smenkhkare's first edict which restored religious plurality, it emphasised that the royal family were now allied to no particular god. And in the years following Akhenaten's Armana interlude, the population needed that type of reassurance. Egypt's people were in no mood to have another bout of state sponsored monotheism forced upon them.

However, the move to Memphis was met with a certain amount of hostility. But this was only from Thebes. Even though the white walled city had long been a civil administrative centre, there was an old religious connection with Ptah. He was the god of craftsmen, creation and rebirth and the town's adopted favourite deity. Ptah was to Memphis what Amun-Re was to Thebes. Although the revitalised priesthood of Karnak knew that it was too early for the royal court to return to Thebes, they still took its move to Memphis as a slight. Ay came close to despair at their attitude. Theoretically, there was nowhere in Egypt for the royal family to live, without giving offence to Thebes. Even the smallest village in the delta had a local god or two, that took precedence over the other deities.

But the Vizier did not despair for long. Instead, he came up with one of his cleverest pieces of bridge building with the estranged Thebans. Shortly after the royal family's arrival in Memphis, the crown prince changed his name. Tutankhaten was no longer the living image of the Aten. Instead, at Ay's bidding he became Tutankhamun or the living image of the Amun. The change to the ninth and tenth letters of his name was crucial. It signified that the years of upheaval, caused by Akhenaten's visions, were over. The royal family wanted to return to their roots in Thebes and would do so when it was safe. Emboldened by this success, the Vizier went a stage further. Akhenaten's daughter Ankhesenpaaten, was renamed Ankesenamun, again reinforcing the Theban connection. Then she was married to the crown prince. This secured Tutankhamun's succession, because he had married into the royal bloodline. Ankhesenamun was more than five years older than her husband and had already reached puberty. Before her father's death at Armana, she had given birth to her child. Even that child's name was changed from Merytaten to Merytamun.

Ay was very pleased with his peace making efforts. He had kept Nakht by his side through this difficult period. Horemheb had returned to the northern frontier just after Akhenaten's entombment in Armana. But Nakht had accompanied the court to Thebes. Nefertiti or Smenkhkare had kept her distance from him. She was polite in conversation, possibly because of his role in placing her on the throne. But that was as far as she went. He did not get even a glimpse of her nature from 10 years ago, when they had briefly been lovers. It was obvious that there was no chance of their affair being rekindled under the new circumstances. Nakht was only slightly saddened by this. He knew that time and events had moved on. The soldier just wished that he was as capable of doing so himself.

One afternoon, shortly before Nakht's own return to active service Ay summoned him. The old man knew about the soldier's imminent departure and wanted to talk to him before he left. But not everything had gone the Vizier's way, since the move to Memphis. He had been joined there by his wife Tiy and the butler Hor, who had left Thebes because of the volatile situation. It was the butler who preceded him into Ay's private rooms. Nakht's eighteen years of service to Ay had not ameliorated the steward's attitude towards him. Hor announced rather sniffily, "Your guest is here, Vizier."

He then gave Nakht a rather disdainful look and left the room. For once Ay was not fiddling with his make up or wig. He was stretched out on his bed and made no effort to rise. Instead, he waved his hand, indicating that the younger man should pull up a chair. While Nakht did so he noticed that his patron looked tired. The efforts of the past six months had obviously taken their toll. As he sat down, he said, "Are you well?"

Slowly propping himself up, the Vizier painfully shook his head from side to side before answering, "Of course I am not well. How could I be, with my wife and her bloody concubine breathing down my neck all day long?" The tone of Ay's voice indicated several, deep draughts of self-pity, which had only been recently consumed. Nakht smiled and took more than a little pleasure at the Vizier's predicament. Ay noted his grin and retorted, "It's all very well for you. You're heading north in a couple of days time. Then you'll be away from it all. Back amongst the army with only the Hittites to worry about. I've got to stay here and try and keep my family from falling out amongst themselves and ruining everything!" Rather gingerly, Ay propped himself up properly on the bed and continued, "My daughter, the King, and her mother, who is my wife, are constantly at each others' throats. My daughter's wife, who also happens to be my grand daughter, believes that she knows better than her own mother – or her husband as she now is. And my step grandson's wife, who is my other grand daughter, thinks she knows more than her sister the Queen. Only her husband, my step grandson, the crown prince, gives me no trouble – yet. That will no doubt come when he gets older. Not even the self satisfied priests of Thebes are so difficult to deal with as the bickering within my family is..."

Nakht let him ramble on and tried to stop smiling. When Ay was ready he would find out the reason for his summons. Having got his complaints off his chest the Vizier appeared to calm down. He rose from his bed and said to Nakht, "I did call you here for a reason, other than sounding off about the royal household. We haven't had a chance to talk alone since those desperate times in Armana. I needed to thank you myself for the work that you did. Together with Horemheb, we saved the Kingdom. Oh…and I also wanted to tell you about your reward!" Ay saw the puzzled expression on the younger man's face and continued,"Yes, your reward. I know that's not a word you have heard very often in your eighteen years of service to me. But I think that by now you have discharged the debt of two golden bars which I paid to your father. So I have decided that if you still want to take a wife, then go ahead and get married. You have my formal permission. Now then, what do you have to say to that?"

Nakht completely stifled not just a grin, but a loud and hearty belly laugh. When Ay had talked about a "reward", he had envisaged being granted a large farm or a country estate. Not being given permission to get married. But seeing that his patron was eagerly awaiting his response he said, "I thank you, Lord Ay. I don't exactly have anybody in mind at the moment. But when I do, you'll be the first to know. That's my promise."

The Vizier beamed from cheek to cheek. His munificence had achieved its desired effect. Nakht's plainly obvious gratitude almost brought tears to his eyes. But Ay had not quite finished and went onto say, "Just one word of caution, my boy. Do not let married life take away your hard edge. I'm more than sure that Egypt will need your special skills and talents, again in the future. And so will I, no doubt!" Ay then fell silent and wandered away from him, towards his dressing table. The audience was apparently over.

Still lost for words, Nakht rose from his chair and prepared to leave the room. As he did so, the soldier momentarily wondered if he had killed the wrong madman in Armana. But before departing, he turned to and Ay and asked, "Vizier, before I go you must answer me one question. Why did you not take the throne for yourself, as we planned for you to do, with Horemheb?"

The older man moved back towards him and staring directly into Nakht's eyes said, "Because it was not yet my time. Think about it, I was too closely associated with the Armana regime to succeed Akhenaten immediately. As nobody had heard of Smenkhkare, until I invented him or her, our current Pharaoh is not tainted by the Aten. But don't worry yourself, my time will come. Nefertiti is aware that she only has possession of the throne for a couple of years. And then, who knows what will happen?"

Rather than attempting to answer that loaded question, Nakht departed and left Ay to his own devices. Two days later he returned to Syria and the service of Horemheb – without a wife.

Chapter Seventeen

Nakht rose early on the last day of the journey to Thebes. Admiral Habt's transport was an excellent vessel, but the atmosphere on board was getting far too claustrophobic for his liking. The northerly wind was fair, so there was no prospect of any rowing to look forward to. The crew cast the boat's moorings off as soon as the light was good enough. By now, the Admiral desperately wanted to get this journey over with and the soldiers away from his ship. Every day his dislike of their Commander had intensified itself several times. Although Nakht was faintly aware of the Admiral's hostility, it didn't concern him in the slightest. Ever since he had arrived in Thebes, as a twelve year old boy, most members of the noble classes had looked down their noses at him. It was something that he had also lived with all his adult life. Besides, there were more important issues for him to worry about. He knew that just after the sunset he would be in the presence of Ay again. It was a prospect that didn't exactly fill him with glee. His patron was now seventy years old and looking every year of his age. Ay had never been the tallest of men, so he had never carried his weight well. In recent years his body had become quite corpulent. And despite the exquisite make up and the expensive wigs that he wore, the ravages of time were plainly etched into his face for all to see. And specifically, one of those ravages was called fear. *More precisely, the fear of his foremost General and erstwhile friend Horemheb...*

...Who had warmly welcomed Nakht back to the northern frontier, following his return from Memphis. The junior officer was never sure as to the sincerity of Horemheb's greetings. In his mind, Nakht had never

forgot the man's attitude on his first journey up the Nile, after leaving Bathar. In the intervening years, although they had served together, nothing approaching friendship had ever materialised. However, in the light of their joint involvement in the death of Akhenaten, he had expected his superior officer to show him a more relaxed approach. But other than his initial greeting it was business as usual. The General soon put him to work in charge of several border patrols. And Nakht was able to lose himself in the never ending struggle against the Hittite's incursions. Until two years, when later he was summoned back to Memphis by Ay.

Smenkhkare and her daughter had occupied the throne for just over two years. As far as Nakht could remember this had been the timetable that Ay had been working to. It was supposed to allow sufficient time for the trauma of Akhenaten's reign to diminish. Although that would never be totally be forgotten or forgiven. Then the royal family were supposed to be safe to return to Thebes. Probably with Ay as Pharaoh, after Nefertiti and Merytamun had abdicated. Well at least that was how Nakht expected events to work out. But when he returned to Memphis, he found that even the Vizier's plans were capable of going astray. Before he left Syria, Horemheb had taken him to one side and advised him that the situation in Memphis was not entirely to Ay's liking. Nakht had been surprised at this display of relative candour from the General. It had also confirmed his suspicions. A summons from Ay could only mean death for somebody and that always came by his hands. But this time Nakht had every intention of getting his own just rewards out of Ay. At the age of thirty one, he was not prepared to find himself fobbed off again with permission to seek a wife or concubine. If the Vizier had further dirty work for him to do, then land and wealth were to be his price this time.

Ay's orders specifically forbade Nakht from attending his private apartments upon his arrival in Memphis. Instead they had instructed the soldier to present himself to the Chief Priest at the temple of Ptah. This was to be done with the utmost secrecy and discretion. Then he was to await Ay's pleasure. This had struck Nakht as intriguing. He quickly deduced that Ay did not want any other members of the royal household to know that he had arrived in Memphis. It also told him that the Vizier had struck up an alliance with Ptah's priesthood. Perhaps the Vizier was not only having problems with his family. It was probable that the creases in his relationship with Thebes had not been entirely smoothed over. So when the soldier reached the white walled city, he quickly made his way to the imposing temple building, where he quietly made himself known. Within a few minutes he was taken by a junior priest, to a lodging house, which was in a not so salubrious part of the city. There he spent the next twenty four hours until Ay finally appeared.

The Vizier was in a strange sort of disguise. For once he was wearing no make up and his wig was made of animal, rather than human hair. Also, Ay's kilt was of the plainest linen and his torso was bare. From his red face and the sweat on his brow, Nakht deduced that he had actually walked to his lodgings. Noting the amused look on Nakht's face, Ay said angrily, "Get off that bed, right now!, I need to lie down. It's almost a quarter of a mile to reach reach your rooms from the temple. I haven't walked anywhere that far in the last twenty years! And then to top it all, I had to negotiate those stairs as well. I swear that my service to this country will be the very death of me."

Nakht vacated his bed and let the Vizier collapse on it. After a few minutes of wheezing. Ay caught his breath and began to explain the reasons behind Nakht's summons to Memphis saying, "Right now I'm supposed to be with the Chief Priest, at the temple, discussing taxation. But don't worry about him. He's on our side. To get away unrecognised, I had to sneak out of the building dressed like a commoner. Now listen, Nakht, we haven't got much time together. I'm due back at the royal residence soon, if I can make it all the way back to the temple, first, on foot. Now you are here because I need you to kill Nefertiti and Merytamun tonight. Is that all right with you...I take it that you will not have a problem with carrying out that task?"

Without hesitation, Nakht answered with six words, "Why do they need to die?"

Ay was not amused by his response. His eyes rolled at the ceiling of Nakht's room and he said, "You dare to ask me why? After all that I have done for you in these past twenty years, you have the bare faced cheek to question me!"

But the soldier was not prepared to take a step back. Ignoring the outburst, he continued, "You took me from Bathar, for which I am grateful. But since then all you have personally given me is permission to marry. When I needed your blessing, before I got involved with your daughter, it was not forthcoming..."

Ay rose from the bed and opened his mouth to speak. But Nakht raised his right hand. The stern expression on his face told the Vizier that he had better keep quiet. "I have killed many men in your service. But what has it got me? Absolutely nothing. All I have is some gold pieces, which were given to me by the Pharaoh that I murdered. You have servants, houses, lands and estates. Other than Hittites to kill in Syria or Palestine, what do I have to my name?"

He paused and watched as Ay carefully considered his words for a moment or two. Eventually, the older man replied, "But my dear boy, I genuinely thought that you were not interested in material things. I believed that all you wanted was a life of action and adventure. You must agree that I have provided that for you..."

"Of course you have," Nakht interjected, "But I am no longer a child. My body will lose its strength one day. Then I will be unable to be a soldier. And what will I have to retire to?"

I take your point. Forgive me, due to the pressures of my office, I have never thought about your future in this way. When all this is over I'll see what I can do. That's a promise. But I do need you to kill Nefertiti and Merytamun tonight..."

"Not good enough," Nakht answered, "Besides you have still not told me why they need to die."

The Vizier placed his head in his hands and then let out a loud yell of exasperation, which Nakht ignored. Seeing that his former protégée was not going to follow his instructions blindly this time, he said, "If you must know they have refused to vacate the throne. I gave them two years of power and we are now well into their third year. They both refuse to abdicate and let Egypt move on. It's a typical mother and daughter alliance. One feeds off the other and neither will listen to reason."

It was Nakht's turn to be silent for a few moments. Then he asked, "Will their abdication be sufficient for you? Despite my differences with Nefertiti, I have no wish to kill her. But I am prepared to do so, provided the right rewards are finally on offer."

"You will be taken to the royal apartments tonight. I am expected there to discuss important matters of state. All the relevant arrangements have been made. Just bring me the crown of Egypt and you will have your estates. Now I must leave from here and return to the temple of Ptah. I am already late."

Ay hurried out of the room, leaving Nakht alone to his thoughts. The Vizier had obviously planned the same ruse that they had successfully worked on Akhenaten. The private meeting, with guards and officials sidelined out of the way. In its wake, an announcement would follow proclaiming the legitimacy of the new King. And then Egypt could get on with her business of living and ruling her colonies. There would be a new direction for the nation, which would be for the better, of course. But there would also be another two dead bodies to dispose of. When that was done Nefertiti and Merytamun might never have existed. The reign of Smenkhkare, Ay's manufactured Pharaoh, would be consigned to dust. Nakht spent the afternoon considering these matters until it was dark. Then Ay's henchman came to lead him to the royal residence. Together they slipped through the narrow streets, until their destination was reached and his guide disappeared into the night.

As Nakht entered the makeshift palace, he noticed that Ay had done his work well. Although there were attendants present they were not military men, just scribes and minor officials. The Vizier's henchman had given him directions to the throne room and a correctly authorised pass. So although he was challenged as a stranger, several times along his way, no suspicions were aroused. Finally he arrived at his destination. But before entering the throne room, at the appointed time of Ay's expected arrival, he stood for a minute and considered his options. Then he showed the doorkeeper his pass and demanded to be allowed to see the Pharaoh. He grinned at Nakht, inferring that he was part of the conspiracy, and gave the soldier passage. Inside the room, Nefertiti and her daughter were sat at a table awaiting the arrival of their father and grandfather respectively.

Nefertiti was the first of the two women to react, as she recognised Nakht immediately. Merytamun was too young to remember him from her days at Armana and didn't see the threat that he posed. But her mother jumped to her feet and shouted animatedly, "What the fuck are you doing here...where is my father, Lord Ay?"

Nakht decided not beat around the bush and said in response, "I'm here to kill you both, Nefertiti. At your father's specific request. And don't bother to summon your bodyguards. It will just be a waste of your breath. They've all been given the evening off. Just like your husband's men were in Armana."

As he finished speaking Nefertiti started to look very worried. Her daughter was confused, but began to appreciate the seriousness of their position when Nakht drew his sword. Both women started to back away from him, but realised that they would be unable to escape him. With his sword drawn Nakht moved towards them and said, "But you do have a choice. Either, I cut you both down in cold blood or you abdicate tonight. It's very simple. Speaking personally, I would go for the latter option. What do you say, Merytamun?"

The younger woman glanced at the sharp edge of Nakht's sword and turned towards her mother saying, "We do not need to die. There are places that we could go and live where nobody knows us. You should have listened to grandfather when he told us it was time to give up the throne!"

Nefertiti ignored her words and hissed at Nakht, "You are only doing this because I threw you over twelve years ago. You were pathetic then and you are even worse now..."

"At least I have never been a pot bellied freak like your husband was," Nakht interrupted, "And for that matter I have never changed my sex, unlike you did! Now what's it going to be? Do I kill you or do we go and see your father?"

"Please, let us go and see grandfather," Merytamun prompted her mother, tugging anxiously on her arm, before Nefertiti could respond. The tone in her voice was desperate for her mother's assent. With great reluctance Nefertiti removed double crown of both Kingdoms from her head and replied, "It looks as if the reign of Smenkhkare is over. I suppose that we'd better go and speak to my father. Although he is a worse bastard than this totally useless cunt who is stood in front of us! No offence meant, Nakht. But I suppose you had to have your revenge against me one day."

The soldier sheathed his sword and said, "Ay wanted you both dead. Those were my orders. But I did not see the need for any more killings. This resolution was my suggestion. Now come it's time to go and see the Vizier and put this matter to rest."

He did not expect any expression of gratitude from Nefertiti and there was none forthcoming. Outside the throne room, the doorman was waiting to lead them to Ay.

Inside his apartments, the two women agreed to leave Memphis that very night, for permanent exile in the far south of Egypt. This was to be in a town called called Kawa, which was in Nubia, between the third and fourth cataracts of the Nile. They readily signed the abdication decree and left to get their belongings together. After they had gone Nakht turned to the Vizier and said, "So now that you are the Pharaoh, how does it feel?"

Ay, who was downing a cup of red wine almost choked on his drink and answered, "I'm not going to be the new King. That honour is still too soon for me to assume. It's the Crown Prince's turn first. Tutankhamun will be the next Pharaoh. Not me. I've still got some old scores to settle with the priests in Thebes, before it's safe for me to take the throne. And there's more than a few debts that I owe to the Ptah priesthood."

Nakht was furious but managed to keet his temper. The old man's intentions had wrong footed him yet again. He said, "And my estate? Tonight I handed you Egypt's crown, just as we agreed, between ourselves in my lodgings. That was what you asked me for and that was exactly what you got. And there was no bloodshed for you to explain to the population at large."

Ay nodded and responded quickly saying, "You did well, Nakht...very well, indeed, to avoid further bloodshed...and I promise that I'll talk to the new Pharaoh, very soon. Rest assured, you have my word on that. But Tuthankhamun's reign can not start with what some ignorant people might call graft or corruption. I'll press your case with him as soon as he is capable of understanding the issues involved."

Nakht was even more irritated by that reply, and answered, "The child is only seven years old. How long do I have to wait until my efforts and contributions to this country are recognised and rewarded?"

Ay seemed genuinely offended by his question. The Vizier visibly shuddered and went on to say, "Your lack of trust disappoints me, truly it does. I had honestly expected far better from you than this, Nakht after everything that I have been done for you. Rather than standing here and insulting my integrity, I suggest you make your preparations to return to Syria. I'm sure that Horemheb's need of your services is far greater than mine is now."

Nakht realised that here was no point in taking the argument any further. The triumphant Ay was now in one of his most devious and irritating moods. He had been recalled to Memphis to do a job. And he had done it in the best possible way. This time there had been no bodies to dispose of. But his solution was still not sufficient for the Vizier to grant him the reward that his years of service merited. So rather then answering the Vizier he walked out of the room in silence. He took the night air for a while, to calm down before returning to his boarding house. As Nakht walked though the streets, he thought to himself that his life might have been easier if he had remained a marsh boy in Bathar. On the way back to his lodgings, he stopped at one of the local bars that remained open all night. He remained there for some time and drank himself into a very drunken stupor.

Chapter Eighteen

At lunch, on the last day of the journey up the Nile, Nakht ordered that wine be served to him instead of beer. He needed fortifying in preparation for his meeting with Lord Ay. But his request did not please the Admiral, who had tolerated the Commander's attitude and low class manners for as long as he could. In response, Habt rose to his feet said to him agitatedly, "For goodness' sakes man! On this vessel we only serve wine when the sun has gone down. What is the matter with you?"

Nakht looked the sailor up and down. Admiral Habt was undoubtedly a high status officer, but in his eyes he was nothing else. And certainly nobody for him to be afraid of. The Admiral's lack of respect and annoyance with Nakht was mutual. The soldier had put up with as much of the Admiral's superior attitude as he could stand. Nakht stood up to his full height and answered, "I would like to take some wine with my meal. If you have wine on board than that should not be a problem. Now you either serve it or I will throw you over the side of your boat. It's entirely up to you. Your decision Admiral..."

To emphasise his words Nakht moved towards the officer, who took the corresponding number of steps backwards. Admiral Habt noticed a distinct reluctance on the part of his crew to come to his assistance. Deciding to try and placate the aggressive soldier, he summoned his orderly saying loudly,
"Bring some wine for Commander Nakht. And be quick about it, man!"

Nakht shook his head slowly from side to side, to the Admiral's alarm. Habt remained puzzled and speechless as the soldier said, "I asked you to serve the wine. Not your orderly. Please be good enough to do as I requested." He then sat down and resumed eating, as the sailor pondered his options. Despite the fact that he had been totally humiliated in front of his less than supportive crew, the Admiral descended into the ship's hold and brought Nakht his wine. With his body shaking, he poured the first measure into the soldier's clay cup. Then he found reason enough to busy himself around the ship, leaving his own lunch unfinished. Nakht sat at the table next to Djar and made a great play of enjoying the wine. But inside himself he was feeling differently. He had just bullied a smaller and weaker man into submission, in front of his naval juniors. There was no real justification for what he had done. Other than the twenty eight years of his life, *that he had spent obeying the orders of the ruling class in Egypt...*

...In the early part of Tutankhamun's reign those orders had come directly from Horemheb. During that time, the General had been a constant presence in Syria. Egypt had maintained a strong military force in the region to deter Hittite incursions. The country had been ruled by three different Pharaohs, in as many years. So, it was vital to show the northern neighbours that the New Kingdom was serious in its intent to protect her territories. But as the threat of invasion temporarily receded, Horemheb found more and more reasons to journey to Thebes. Although the new Pharaoh and his Queen had been crowned in Memphis, shortly afterwards. Ay had moved the royal court back to Thebes. This was only achieved at a great cost to the treasury. Firstly, the debt to the Memphis priesthood had to be paid. It took the form of a large extension to the temple of Ptah. And secondly, Ay's bridge building with the Theban priesthood had to continue. So at the temples at Karnak and Luxor, the construction works

started by Amenhotep III and halted by his son, resumed. A further temple to the far south at Kawa was also started. This was their price for offering Nefertiti and Merytamun sanctuary.

While these works were taking place, Horemheb flitted back and forth between Thebes and the Northern frontier. Although Nakht was no politician, he could see that the general's position was getting stronger by the day. With Ay acting as regent for the young Pharaoh, his mind was removed from his military roots. This process had started many years previously, when he had become Akhenaten's Master of Horses. At the same time Horemheb had maintained the impetus of his own military career. He had also cemented his political links by marrying Ay's daughter Mutnodjme. So the General had a foot in both camps and more importantly was now more able to deliver the army than the Vizier was. This gave him a very strong influence and led to him becoming co-regent, with Ay, in all but name. Horemheb emphasised this to Nakht after one of his trips to Thebes. Knowing of his subordinate's lack of wealth and the broken promises that he had suffered from Ay, he called him to one side. To Nakht's surprise, Horemheb informed him that the soldier was now officially a member of the royal household. His General had taken the trouble of listing him as a military officer, attached to the court. It was something than Ay should have done, but had not previously bothered to do. Nakht was pleased about his direct superior's official recognition of himself, although he was slightly concerned about Horemheb's motives. He didn't know where he would stand if the General was seeking to attempt a coup against power of the Vizier.

There was also one other important factor that counted against Ay – his age. He was now into his early sixties, where as Horemheb was just turned forty. The

General was at an age where he could be a far more vigorous and attentive man than his older friend. Without the strains of daily court life and the Theban priests to deal with, he was able to gather support and strengthen his hand. And it now seemed as if this included getting Nakht on his side. Being a member of the royal household, gave the soldier an income and a position which, until then, had been denied him. This was by no means the estates or houses that Nakht had expected from Ay. But it was something tangible and far better than just working for his bed and board. It was with interest that Nakht sat back and awaited his next summons to Ay's presence. This did not come for two more years, until the fifth year of Tutankhamun's reign. It came after two successful campaigns in the south of the empire against Nubian insurrections. Horemheb had been placed in charge of the Egyptian forces and their mercenaries. Unlike Nakht's previous expedition to Kush under Ay, the actions had been fully blown military affairs. After some vicious fighting, the revolts were ruthlessly crushed and Egypt's supply of gold from the south was assured. As a result the General's standing with the populace and the military rose even higher. It was against this backdrop that Nakht was summoned to Thebes.

    The royal court had returned to the palace of Malkata. As Nakht's ship moored on the western bank of the Nile, he had noticed that the eastern bank looked very busy. Tuthankhamun's programme of building works was well under way and offering employment to most people who moved back to the city. Once off the boat, he made his way to the palace. Ay had not chosen to meet with him in his own residence, preferring the location of Malkata itself. The soldier was now thirty five years of age and found it hard to think that it was twenty three years since he had first trodden than route.

But some things never changed. Once he had negotiated the palace's precincts, Nakht came face to face with the butler Hor. The Vizier had obviously installed him in the palace away from Tiy. Age had not changed him, other than physically. With the look of a man who had just stepped barefoot into a soggy cow's turd, he took the soldier to Ay's quarters.

It was almost five years since Nakht had last seen the Vizier in Memphis. To his surprise, Ay's appearance had changed very little. His corpulence and other signs of ageing seemed to be under control. After Hor had announced Nakht's arrival, the Vizier looked up from the papyrus that he was studying and said, "Nakht, my dear boy! It has been so long since our last meeting. Forgive me for neglecting you and tell me how are you keeping?"

"I am keeping almost as well as you are. You don't seemed to have aged a day since Memphis."

Ay managed a broad grin before replying, "My royal duties keep me fit. There's no rest for the wicked in Thebes. But in honour of your visit, I have decided to take an afternoon off. We shall go to the palace's lake where we shall be wined and dined in style. And then you can tell me all about Horemheb and his growing influence in the army."

Nakht smiled to himself. He had expected instructions to kill somebody. But it seemed as if this particular summons related only to Ay's need for gossip about Horemheb. Although as they sat outdoors, by the artificial lake which Amenhotep III had built, the soldier was not prepared to let his patron off the hook so lightly. When the slaves had served them with the finest food and drink that Egypt could offer Nakht said, "Now that our Pharaoh is twelve years old, have you had a chance to press my case for for a reward?"

"I've done more than that," Ay retorted almost choking on his food, "You have been on the payroll of the royal household for the last three years. Surely there can be no greater reward than that. The clerks have maintained a ledger on your behalf. When you finally leave the army, I'm more than sure that your retirement will be well provided for!"

The soldier grinned at his response. Horemheb had claimed the credit for his inclusion on the list and Nakht had no reason to disbelieve him. Now Ay was attempting to make out that his was his doing. And he had every reason to mistrust the Vizier. But before he could find the words to answer Ay, the Vizier said with great purpose, "But enough of such trivialities. Tell me, what is Horemheb saying behind my back?" As always the older man easily found a way to change the thrust of the conversation, when it involved Nakht's prospects.

Out of loyalty to his long time patron Nakht said, "He has the army in his pocket. But, I suppose you must have known that already."

"Of course I did and some time ago. My faculties are not so diminished as to prevent me from realising the facts. Obviously, a serving senior officer will be far more able to insinuate himself with the military hierarchy than my role permits me to do. Especially after the army's victories in Nubia..." Ay's voice tailed off and a wistful expression flickered across his face. Nakht was unsure as to what he should say. His own preferment had been dealt with and was now off limits.

But as Ay was now silent and looking rather crestfallen he said, "I have heard of no plots against yourself from Horemheb or any other person. Of course I am no politician, but my ears are still good. In my opinion, the General is happy with the current political position. He is building his support base within the army. But I do not believe that he poses a threat to you – yet."

His final word brought Ay to life as he replied, "Yet! You said "yet". Horemheb is manoeuvring himself into a position where he can and will be a threat to me. I realise all of this, but at the moment I just don't know what to do about it!"

Nakht wanted to say that the Vizier could do more to reward his supporters, rather than constantly lying to them. Then he would have a stronger and more loyal retinue to call upon. But he held his tongue and tucked into the picnic lunch that the servants had provided them with. As the conversation turned more to generalities, rather than specifics, Ay recovered his good humour. He even ribbed Nakht about the fact that he had not yet taken a wife. When the picnic was finally finished, the two men parted on the best of terms. The Vizier could be the finest of companions – when he chose to be. Nakht returned to the Nile transport for his journey north. He knew, as he had done for some time, that Ay would keep him perpetually dangling on a string. His rewards and preference were always going to be held in abeyance. They would never be delivered. As long as his patron had use for him nothing would materialise. And the reverse was true of the Vizier's personal attention. Until Ay was in a difficult spot the Commander would cease to exist. So another four years, without any substantial improvement in his circumstances, passed before Nakht received his next summons from Ay.

Chapter Nineteen

Aboard his Nile transport, Admiral Hapt had kept out of Nakht's way for the whole of the afternoon. He had decided that upon returning to Thebes, he would make an official complaint about the army Commander's behaviour. Nobody had the right to humiliate him in front of his crew in such a manner. Especially somebody who belonged to the marginal classes of Egyptian society. In his opinion the hierarchy should not allow such people to prosper. If it did, then it was time to hand the country over to the Hittites, the Nubians or even the sea people. Without discipline and respect for position, the whole of the New Kingdom's social order was at stake. He might not be able to take Nakht on in a fist fight, but he certainly intended to give a good account of himself at the Commander's court martial. After he had made his complaint, Habt was in no doubt that his superiors would insist upon the Commander's immediate arraignment. Discipline must be seen to prevail by the lower classes and transgressions needed to be punished severely (in the Admiral's opinion, at least).

Nakht on the other hand had almost totally forgotten about the Admiral existence and his petty complaints. As far as the soldier was concerned Habt was a total irrelevance. By nightfall the crown of Egypt would be secured in Ay's favour. So the Admiral had ceased to matter and was an irrelevance. The boat was going to arrive in Thebes, in accordance with his schedule. If he had been a vindictive man, then later that night he would ask Ay to feed the Admiral to the crocodiles. But he wasn't – so the thought didn't even cross his mind. Instead he gave thought to the reason why Ay had summoned him again, *some five years after their picnic lunch in the palace gardens at Malkata...*

...It had been a long and exhausting five years for the Commander. Egypt's recent campaigns against the Hittites had not gone as well as those against the Nubians had. Northern incursions had continually grown stronger and more well directed. Some border territories in Syria had become too difficult to defend and land had been given up. Nakht and the men under his command, which now included Djar, had not taken a step back. But other detachments of the army were not half so resolute or defiant. So they had been forced to fall back, away from the Euphrates, with the rest of their comrades. General Horemheb's stock at court had fallen as a result of these reverses. Although he was still regarded as the co-regent alongside Ay, power had shifted back towards the Vizier. Although, this had not all gone entirely in Ay's favour. Nakht had heard from Horemheb about the rise of a creature called Tutu. The soldier had encountered him at court, but always chose to avoid his company. Tutu was not an Egyptian, being from Palestine. He had initially ingratiated himself with Amenhotep III and then with Akhenaten. Now he had now succeeded in doing the same with Tutankhamun. Horemheb had expressed the view that the young King was listening more to Tutu than his fellow countrymen. Nakht's dislike of the courtier was not founded out of racism towards the Palestinians, but out of a mistrust of the man's motives. From the first time that he had been introduced to him in Armana, the soldier had felt that he was in the presence of something very dirty and extremely slimy.

So Nakht returned to Thebes, at Ay's request. He was five years older and not very much wiser, in his own opinion. And he was certainly no richer. Nakht had been summoned to Ay's estate, rather than the palace of

Malkata. To his surprise there was no sign of Hor, as he made his way to the Vizier. An unknown young attendant presented him to the old man. And "old" was now the appropriate word to describe Ay. He had turned seventy earlier in the year and was looking his age. Whether this was due to the ageing process or the intrigues at court, Nakht was interested to find out. But by way of conversation he asked, "Where's your butler Hor? I was looking forward to seeing his supercilious features."

Ay smiled at the question and replied, "His tomb is but a few miles from here. You can visit it tomorrow, if you really want to. I do sometimes, just to cheer myself up and ensure that he is finally gone. Although it never actually works, because it makes me realise that I must have paid that man far too much. The artwork on his tomb's walls was painted by master craftsmen. Almost all of it was done freehand and you know how bloody expensive that is to commission. What a resting place for a mere butler!"

"And how did your dear wife take this sad loss to the household?"

"A lot worse than I did, my boy. You have my assurance about that. But I did not summon you here to discuss his less than sad demise. nfortunately, I have more work for you to do. Yet again, the future of our dear country is at stake..."

Nakht had only one word to say and he said it loudly, "Bollocks!"

Ay bit his bottom lip and then continued, "I thought you might say something of that nature. Now you have done your country some great services in the past..."

"I will say bollocks to you again," Nakht interjected, "I've already delivered the crown to you twice. And both times you were too afraid to take it.

Now, you obviously want me to secure it for you for a third time. Otherwise, I would still be serving with Horemheb in what's left of what we own Syria. But if you want my help, then this time I want payment in advance. No more promises that evaporate like the Nile's mists in the early morning sun. Have I made myself clear?"

The Vizier nodded, almost sincerely, and responded, "If you can pull this off, then you can have my entire estate in Malkata. That's how serious things are. I'll even call a scribe right now and to draw up a legally binding document, if you want. But Nakht, you must accept my word. The future of Egypt needs to be handled in great secrecy at this most delicate of times."

"So tell me about it," Nakht replied, with a firm and measured tone in his voice. He then added, "But not before your servants have brought me some of your finest wines to drink!"

Ay rose from his seat and summoned Hor's replacement to bring some wine. When the young man had served the wine and then departed, Ay resumed, "There are at least three problems, if not more. The first relates to the Pharaoh himself. Tutankhamun is now almost seventeen years of age. And under the influence of his wife, Ankhesenamun, he is becoming more difficult to handle by the day."

"In what way?" Nakht asked, after taking a sip of wine from his cup.

"In every way," Ay retorted, "Because he was brought up in Armana, Tutankhamun still overtly worships the Aten. He has recently had some carvings made of his coronation. They show our young Pharaoh alongside Ankhesenamun, his Great Wife, basking in the radiance of the solar disc. Just like his father before him did with my daughter. Even his golden throne bear the profane images. Now that he is reaching the age of majority, I fear that the country could be plunged into turmoil again. And there's more as well..." This time it was Ay's turn to take a sip from his cup, before resuming, "... Two months ago he had his father's mummy removed from its tomb in Armana and reburied in the Valley of the Kings. Apparently he didn't want it destroyed by the tomb robbers and desecraters who now operate unchecked in Armana. What do you think that the priesthood of Thebes thought and had to say about that?"

Nakht considered Ay's words briefly and answered, "I doubt that they were over impressed. But what is the third problem?"

Ay needed little or no prompting and said, "It's that treacherous little arsehole, Tutu. You know the bastard Palestinian. All of this is his doing, because it is his opinion that the Pharaoh has been listening to. Besides, I have evidence that Tutu had suppressed calls for assistance from Egyptian settlers in his homeland during Akhenaten's reign Of course Tutankhamun's wife doesn't help matters, but no daughter of mine or Akhenaten ever did. So I want you to kill the Pharaoh and blame it on Tutu. That will put the little, northern shit out of commission. After they are both out of the way I will take the throne!"

"And the King's great wife, what about her?"

"Let's leave her alone for the time being. As a princess of royal blood, she could be useful to us once her husband and Tutu are taken care of."Ay then scratched his lip for a moment, before saying, "I don't want Tutankhamun killed outright and certainly not by a sword blow. The political situation is such that it must be blamed on Tutu. And it would help me greatly if he were to linger for a while. Just to give me a chance to put my plans into action."

"That will be difficult," Nakht countered.

"Not for a man of your refined talents. To make matters easier, I have assigned you to take command of the King's guard. Of course one or two eyebrows were raised at that. Now you can appreciate why we must not be suspected in any way."

The Vizier then dismissed Nakht to give him time to think. On the following day the soldier was to take up his new duties at the palace. Ay had given him a week to familiarise himself with the Pharaoh's and Tutu's routine. And then a week to achieve the desired result. That night Nakht thought long and hard. Not just about how he was going to achieve his aim, but why he was going to attempt it. He had no doubt that Ay's promise of his estate at Malkata would prove to be as brittle a promise as his others had been over the years. It wasn't as if killing people gave him a thrill or any enjoyment. Since despatching the badly wounded Nubian soldier in Kush, Nakht had grown to accept that killing other human beings was an integral part of his life. His only justification for his actions came back to the fact that he loved his country. And if the Pharaoh or any other person threatened Egypt's stability then he would kill them. It wasn't to further Ay's career or even his own prospects. They had never been advanced greatly despite his years of service to the crown. No, it came down to one specific issue – he had never and would never kill a person who was not an enemy of his homeland. That was why he had spared Nefertiti and her daughter in Memphis. Other than masquerading as Smenkhkare, beyond her pre-agreed time, she had presented no real threat to Egypt's stability.

Nakht's transition to his new role in charge of the King's guard seemed to meet with little hostility in the court. He assumed that this was because the new generation of courtiers regarded him as Horemheb's creature rather than Ay's. Within two days he had worked out a plan to meet the Vizier's specifications. And it would be quite easy to put into operation. That was because Tutankhamun had made one very big mistake. By taking Tutu into his confidence, the courtier had been promoted to head of his personal household. This meant that each morning the King met with him on his own, in the royal apartments. There they would discuss the issues of the day out of the hearing of the other palace officials. Even members of the King's bodyguard were prohibited from being present at these conferences. So the two men were totally alone together. A part of Nakht wondered if the King was actually Tutu's catamite, as the older courtier was well known for his homosexual tendencies. But be that as it may, their secluded meeting gave him the ideal alibi. When the daily liaison was concluded, Tutankhamun would be on his own and Tutu would be the last person to have been officially in his chambers. It seemed to be too good an opportunity to miss. And once the first week of Nakht's new role had elapsed his mind was made up.

However, the second part of Ay's plan caused him more concern. How to inflict a mortal wound that would not be immediately fatal? For a time, he considered the use of poison, but decided against it. It would be far too difficult to force the King to drink the potion and would give him the chance to raise the alarm. After much thought an idea came to him. A blow to the back of the head. Although this had two potential setbacks. If Nakht hit the diminutive Pharaoh too hard he would die instantly. Conversely, if he struck the blow too softly then Tutankhamun would only be knocked unconscious. Then when the King woke up, provided he didn't have amnesia, the game would be up. It was all a matter of correctly judging his not inconsiderable strength. Ever the perfectionist, Nakht decided that he must put himself to the test, before undertaking the mission for real. To this end he arranged to Ay to have some slightly built, condemned criminals taken to the cellars of his estate at Malkata. This was done under conditions of strictest secrecy, at the end of his first week back in Thebes. On his day off, under the watchful gaze of Ay, he practised on the bound convicts. It only took him three goes to judge the strength required. The first man was killed outright, his spinal cord snapped by the impact. So he tempered his blows on the second criminal. He was repeatedly knocked unconscious, until Nakht lost his patience and snapped the man's neck. Finally, he judged his blow correctly and put the third man into a coma that lasted for twenty four hours, after which time Ay had him suffocated. Nakht did not feel too badly about killing the men, as they had already been sentenced to die for their crimes.

    A few days after this experiment he stood outside the King's bedchamber with two of his men. Tutu was inside the room with the Pharaoh, having his daily discussion with the King. Their meeting dragged on slightly longer than was usual and the soldier became anxious. But he needn't have worried. A few minutes later and the effeminate courtier emerged looking very pleased with himself, although his brow was sweaty. Nakht imagined that his latest lies and calumnies must have gone down well with Tutankhamun. As Tutu closed the bedchamber's door and started to walk down the corridor, the Commander said to his soldiers, "I don't like this. Did you notice his sweaty brow? That man was in there for far too long. I now fear for the King's welfare. You must go quickly and detain him, while I check on his majesty!"

    "But sir, he is the head of…"

    "I don't care who he is. Not even Amun will help us if our Pharaoh has been hurt…just obey your orders!"

The soldiers saw the concerned look on the Commander's face and set off to apprehend Tutu.

This gave Nakht the chance that he needed. He slipped quickly into Tutankhamun's apartments, completely startling the naked Pharaoh, who was reclining face down on a coach. To Nakht's total amazement, he saw that his King was wiping his buttocks clean, with a white linen cloth. So it looked as if Tutankhamun had been Tutu's catamite, as Nakht had half suspected But before the King could say a single word, the Commander hauled him to his feet and span him round. The slenderly built youth was unable to offer even token resistance to the older man's greater strength. Tutankhamun now had his back to him. Remembering that the seventeen year old was much weaker than the criminals he had practised on, Nakht delivered a measured uppercut to the base of his skull. Tutankhamun collapsed onto the marbled floor. If he ever awoke, then the Commander's life was over. Although if he didn't, then Ay had the prize that he had coveted all his life. But time was now of the utmost importance.

Leaving the comatose King, Nakht swiftly ran out of the royal apartments He headed straight towards his men, who had detained an irate Tutu some distance down the corridor. As he remonstrated with them, Nakht yelled,
"Bind him and then quickly summon the physicians. The Pharaoh lies unconscious in his room. This evil traitor has just tried to murder him!"

The soldiers needed no second bidding. As his hands were tied, Tutu protested his innocence loudly saying, "The King was alive when I left his room...you are speaking total nonsense..."

"It is thanks to Amun that the King is still alive," Nakht interjected, "I'm pleased to say that your attempted assassination has failed."

Tutu looked on the Commander with absolute horror in his eyes. And then the truth dawned on him. All the colour drained from his face, as he said, "You've tried to kill him. Not me. It was you!"

"If I want to kill a man then he dies. That is my job and I would look forward to doing it to you, for your treachery."

At Tutu's trial, which Ay presided over, Nakht was the main witness. Great play was made of the fact that neither he or his men had heard the King's voice, when Tutu had left the room. The Vizier also disclosed his proof of Tutu's machinations against Egypt during the reign of Akhenaten. Tutu's defence was that Nakht had tried to kill the Pharaoh on Ay's instructions. But the fact that the soldier was officially listed as an officer to Horemheb, rather than Ay, discredited that argument. The accusations of Tutu's previous treachery, his foreign birth and blatant homosexuality were all held against the courtier. Allied to his general unpopularity, the court (Ay in fact) could bring in only one verdict. He was found guilty and sentenced to death. While all of this was happening Tutankhamun hovered between life and death in a coma. Despite the best medical care that Egypt could provide, he died of a brain haemorrhage three months later. That was two months after Tutu was impaled on a stake for the attempt on the Pharaoh's life. The execution took place in the precincts of the temple of Monthu in Karnak. Nakht did not attend.

Chapter Twenty

It was early evening when the Nile transport finally docked in Thebes, to the relief of both Admiral Hapt and Nakht. The former still intended to make a strongly worded complaint to his superiors. But the latter was just relieved to be out of the claustrophobic atmosphere of the ship. Neither man exchanged even the simplest of pleasantries as the soldiers disembarked. On the dock side, Nakht had Djar assemble the men. The detail was two members short, but the Commander was sure that they would be safe in Gosa. He would make arrangements for their return to Thebes, the next time a transport was due to dock in Avaris. Without any prompting, his second in command gave him the smelly and soiled bag containing Zannanza's severed hand. Then Nakht told the detail to fall out and enjoy their first night back in Thebes. Leaving them to go about their business, he thanked Djar for his support and walked towards Ay's estate at Malkata. It was still the Vizier's property, rather than his. Despite the old man's promises, following the death of Tutankhamun, *no scribe had ever been summoned to write the document that would transfer the estate to Nakht...*

...It was far too soon for that to take place, Ay had insisted and his arguments were initially persuasive. They had only just got away with mortally wounding Tutankhamun. If the Vizier's enemies, of which there were plenty, had even the slightest sniff of him making such a generous gift to Nakht, then people would start to talk. Besides, hadn't his lack of generosity stood both them in very good stead at Tutu's trial? Horemheb was still officially listed as the soldier's patron. That needed to remain the case while the dust settled. There were far too many suspicious minds in Thebes, for Ay to even

think about incriminating himself. The list went on and on, increasing by the day and sounding less logical as time passed. Despite Tutu's execution at the temple of Monthu, Amun's Chief Priest had looked at the Vizier in a strange way one morning. So the man obviously suspected something. There was no way that this overt accusation could be given any solid evidence to base itself upon. Each time the Vizier brushed him off, Nakht smiled to himself. He had expected nothing more from Ay and was almost pleased not to be disappointed.

But there was one serious cloud on the Vizier's horizon. His grand daughter Ankhesenamun, the late Pharaoh's wife. Ay had spared her for one reason. He wanted to marry her. When he assumed the crown it would only be legitimised if he married into the royal bloodline. And this was best epitomised by Tutankhamun's widow. Except that the young woman had refused to even consider the prospect of taking the seventy year old Ay as her husband. Nakht had a great deal of sympathy for her. She was only twenty three years old and had suffered a great deal in her life. At the age of thirteen she had bore her father, Akhenaten, a child. Then she had lived through the turmoil at the end of the Armana experiment, to be renamed and married to her brother. In the course of their marriage she had experienced two miscarriages of fully formed foetuses. Finally, her younger husband had been taken from her by his own hand, albeit on Ay's bidding. Although Nakht felt few self recriminations about the act, the royal couple had been genuinely fond of each other. Even if her husband had sought carnal pleasure with Tutu. And now her grandfather was telling her that she was to be his bride. So she refused and set about proving that she had inherited more from Ay's side of the family than Akhenaten's. But because of her youth and lack of experience, she made mistakes. In the same way that her dead husband had exposed himself by his relationship with Tutu, Ankesenamun exposed herself by calling on the services of a scribe. Fortunately for Ay, who was already starting to act like the Pharaoh, it was a scribe loyal to him. Although the young widow was literate, this only extended as far as her native Egyptian language. The plan to outwit her grandfather, required somebody who was capable of writing in the cuneiform script that the Hittites used. The mistake she made was to choose the wrong scribe. Just after her husband's death, she had a clay tablet inscribed that was sent to the Hittite King Suppiluliumas. Her scribe brought the tablet straight to Ay, before it was passed to the Hittite ambassador.

     The message contained an intriguing and explosive proposal. Ankesenamun requested the King to send her a royal prince to be her husband, as she had no son to take care of her. Simply put, Tutankhamun's widow was offering the throne of Egypt to the Hittites. She also complained bitterly about the fact that she was being forced to marry a servant. This was a less than thinly veiled reference to Ay's proposal of marriage. Ay ordered the scribe to make a copy and then pass the original to the Hittite ambassador. He then alerted his own spies in their embassy and awaited King Suppiluliumas's reply. This was initially in the negative. The old man could not believe the offer from the very heart of his sworn enemy. He thought it was a joke or a trap and replied accordingly to his ambassador. But when he received Ankhesenamun's second request, backed up by confirmation of her sincerity from the Hittite ambassador, he decided that she was being serious. Unable to believe his luck at the prospect of inheriting his enemy's Kingdom, he despatched his son Zannanza to Egypt. Ay having been informed about all of this, by both his spies and Ankhesenamun's scribe, had sent Nakht to Syrian border to dispose of the prince and bring proof of his demise.

Which was why Nakht was walking to the Vizier's residence at Malkata, carrying a linen bag containing the dead Zannanza's right hand. He knew that the old schemer would be pleased to see him, despite his protestations to the Admiral. A difficult mission had been accomplished and within a given time scale. But what intrigued the soldier more than anything was how Ay would play things from this point on. His experience told him that it should be interesting to observe, if nothing else. Inside the Vizier's home he was greeted by the new butler, Tchay. Unlike his predecessor, Tchay treated Nakht with respect and civility. With a minimum of ceremony, he led the Commander to Ay's personal study. Inside the room, Nakht was surprised to see that General Horemheb had preceded him in making the journey north.

The two men rose to their feet as he joined them. Ay poured a measure of wine into a third cup and said, "My lookouts told me that your vessel had been seen on the approach to Thebes. I take it that things went well for our cause?"

Puzzled by Horemheb's presence, which he had not expected, Nakht did not reply. Instead, he placed the soiled bag on Ay's table and took up his beaker of wine. The Vizier stared at his gift and said, "I assume that is my wedding present. Now do you still have the clay tablet in your possession?"

"No. You'll find it nestled against the prince's hand. I put it in there as I walked up from the river."

Horemheb, who had sat down, rose to his feet again and stated, "Nakht, you have done really well. Hasn't he, Ay? The last piece of the puzzle is now in place. Don't you think it's time to go and see the Queen?"

Ay beamed fulsomely and replied, "Once my boy has finished his wine. The night is yet young and we now have time on our side. By the way, Nakht, how did you get on with the Admiral and when can I expect his official letter of complaint?"

The Commander finished his swig of wine and answered, "You should get it within two days. Once the idiot has worked out how to put ink to papyrus!"

"You should really do something about that sailor," Horemheb cut in, before the Vizier could speak, "He's an old woman of the worst type. Now, Nakht, are you ready for another drink?"

Not one to refuse extra lubrication, the soldier accepted the offer. When the jug of wine was finished Ay led them to the palace, which was only a short walk away. On the way there, Horemheb explained to Nakht that he had been summoned from Syria at Ay's command. The Vizier wanted Ankhesenamun to know that the army was behind him. Inside the palace it took some time for them to be allowed to see the widowed Queen. But Ay insisted that he had a matter of national security to discuss, which would not wait until the morning. On a personal basis Nakht knew that it was a difficult time for her. Not only was she expecting a new husband to arrive from the north, but it was time for her dead husband's entombment. Almost eighty days had elapsed since his death and the mummification process was complete. All that remained was the last few days of the religious rituals. Then he would be laid to rest in the Valley of the Kings. So the last thing that she wanted to see that night was Ay and his two companions.

The three men were reluctantly admitted into her chambers, where she was surrounded by attendants. Nakht assumed that she had decided upon safety in numbers. Ankhesenamun was similar in build and appearance to her dead husband. Physically, she was a delicate and slightly built woman, who had the same sexless features of all of Akhenaten's children. But she definitely had her grandfather's mind. Her visitors were left in no doubt about that as she welcomed them by saying, "Vizier Ay, if you have come to press your attentions upon me at this sad time then they are more unwelcome than ever. And even though you bring your General and his chief assassin to my private chambers, you will not change my mind!"

Ay pondered and paced around the large room for a few moments before saying, "Alas, my dear lady. If it was only that simple. Then we would be gone in an instant and I would never trouble you again. But I have evidence of a Hittite spy ring that permeates the highest level of Egyptian society. Some might call it a plot, against the state. But before I can give you proof, you must dismiss your attendants. My information is that sensitive..."

"What, so your killer can murder me without any witnesses...do you think I am that stupid Ay?" was her retort.

Horemheb, who until then had been standing silently in the background, suddenly said with purpose, "We can disclose our findings in their presence. But that will only lead to their deaths, as they cannot hear what we have to say and live. As for yourself, perhaps you recall certain exchanges of communications which you recently made with our enemies the Hittites..."

"That is enough!" Ankhesenamun quickly countered, as she looked up at her retinue and shouted, "You are all dismissed. I need to talk to my Vizier, General and their chief assassin alone. So get out now, everyone of you and give me some privacy!"

As the startled servants left the room, Nakht stepped forward. He ignored Ankhesenamun's look of loathing and opening the bag, turned it upside down over her bed. Zannanza's shrivelled hand and the clay tablet dropped onto the clean linen. The young woman stared at the two objects and said, "If you are trying to frighten me then it will not work!" As no one replied, she stared directly at Ay and continued, still confident, "You at least should know that I am made of far sterner stuff, grandfather..."

Ay let her final word tail off, before picking up the clay tablet and stating,
"I do not read this Hittite script very well. But I know people who do, like the scribe you entrusted to write it on your behalf. I may be an unwelcome servant in your eyes, but at least I serve only one country – Egypt."

Ankhesenamun's confidence started to evaporate and her face turned white with fear. Her reply was hesitant and brief, "It's a forgery."

Ay nodded at her words and then took up the severed hand. He presented it to her and continued, "Here. is all that remains of your Hittite prince. The one that you summoned from old King Suppiluliumas. I believe his name was Zannanza. My boy Nakht ensured that the buzzards got the rest of him. But we decided to keep this bit for you. Look at his signet ring. Were you to understand their writing, then you would see his initial inscribed upon it. So he will not be coming to rescue you." The young woman's already white face turned to a deadlier shade of pale. But Ay was not prepared to let matters rest and said, "Of course the Commander interrogated him before his death. Tell her what happened in the desert, Nakht."

"I placed the clay tablet before his eyes and spoke your name," the soldier responded looking directly at the Queen, "He tried to deny it a language that I do not know, but his eyes told a different story. Then I killed him..."

"Like you killed my husband, you dirty bastard and then lied about poor Tutu at his trial!"

Ay let her finish before imposing himself again by saying, "Unlike the members of my beloved royal family, Nakht's parentage is not in doubt. But if your former husband was capable of bearing children, then I have no doubt that he would now be carrying Tutu's child. That is, were he still to be alive. But you tell her te full truth, Nakht. The time for pleasantries has long since passed."

The soldier stepped forward and swallowed. Then he stated, "He was wiping Tutu's fluids from his anus when I entered the bedchamber. That was the reason for their private meeting every morning."

Ankhesenamun burst into tears at this latest revelation. Pharaohs were not known for their monogamous nature. But for a woman to know that the husband she had loved had been taking another man's cock up his arse was too much for her to bear. Ay, however, did not relent and took up the conversation, "Now bear in mind that we are virtually at war with King Suppiluliumas. So do you really think that your offer of our country's throne will be well received by the public at large? If you do, then I will believe you to be a bigger fool than your father. Treason has a rather bad ring to it these days. But there is another way out, grand daughter. Accept my proposal of marriage. Then all of this unpleasantness can be put to one side and you can get on with your young life."

The Vizier then gestured to Nakht and Horemheb to remain silent. Eventually, Ankesenamun stopped her tears and said, "If I marry you then this will all be forgotten? And you promise not to trouble me as a man does to his wife?"

Ay nodded and replied, "Of course not. Ours is to be merely a marriage of convenience – for the greater good of Egypt. It will be nothing more and nothing less. Please be assured of that. You have my promise there."

She was still unsure as to whether or not to accept Ay's words. But the young woman had no real choice in the matter. So, she answered with great reluctance, "Go and make the arrangements. I suppose that I can bury one husband and marry another within the week. Just keep your filthy killer out of my presence. I do not want to see him in court again!"

On the way out of the palace, Ay was in an elated and rather strange jovial mood. He said excitedly to Horemheb, "Tomorrow, I will commission the painter to add the blue crown to my image in Tutankhamun's tomb. Posterity will now know me as the Pharaoh that succeeded him."

The General grinned at his words and answered, "And I suppose that you will also claim Tutankhamun's building works as your own. Seriously, Ay at your age, you do not have long left to stamp your mark on our country."

The new Pharaoh in waiting did not take his words the wrong way and said, "Oh don't worry about that. This old dog has still got some life left in him. Then it will be your turn, provided everything goes to plan. Give me two years and you will be my co-regent. And as for you Nakht, you shall have your reward. Once the crown is placed on my head, I will have the power to do you justice."

Nakht didn't exactly believe this statement and made a mental note not to hold his breath. Especially as he could recall Ankhesenamun's words about banishing him from court. The soldier replied, "Right now, I'd settle for a large cup of wine. In my humble opinion, it's much easier on the soul to kill people, rather than to try and reason with them. Don't you think?" Neither Ay or

Horemheb chose to reply and the three men continued their return journey in silence, after his comment.

Chapter Twenty One

That night Nakht slept well, by his standards, in a full sized bed at Ay's residence. Being able to stretch out in comfort made a welcome change to the restricting confines of the naval hammock. But he still woke in the middle of the night, despite his luxurious bedroom. Ay had given him a pitcher of wine to take to his room. After several cups, the Commander felt relaxed enough to return to his bed. Although sleep would not come. When Nakht closed his eyes, he saw images of his victims. There was Zannanza with his lacerated throat, dropping dead into the desert sand, before his hand was severed. This was followed by a picture of Akhenaten breathing his last and falling out of his clasp, to the floor in Armana. And then he saw Tuthankhamun's unconscious form sliding onto a marbled floor in Thebes, after the his well delivered mortal blow. Even the three condemned men that he had killed in Ay's cellars appeared to taunt him. They were accompanied by various other Egyptians, Nubians, Palestinians and Hittites, whose angry words he could not comprehend. Harkhaf, his old watch commander from the Valley of the Kings, also put in a brief appearance. Clutching at the wooden spike that had impaled him, the ghost's eyes stared directly at the army officer. As far as Nakht was concerned, the only things missing were a pink crocodile or a brightly spotted hippopotamus. He had seen those strangely coloured beasts before after drinking excessively, but had not previously seen the spirits of those that he had killed.

It took a supreme effort of will for him to go down to breakfast, the following morning. The perceptive and attentive Tchay noticed that Nakht seemed troubled. After seating the Commander, he brought him a plate of food and served Nakht personally. It was nothing like the treatment that the Commander was used to from the butler's predecessor, Hor. But Ay and Horemheb who were already seated, were oblivious to the junior man's physical condition, being full of political intrigue. The new Pharaoh's coronation was to be held in the temple of Karnak, before Tutankhamun's funeral. Then Ay would be able to officiate at that sad event and duly emphasise his legitimacy. A simple marriage ceremony to Ankhesenamun, was to take place that day in Malkata at the royal palace. It was at that point that the two men took note of Nakht. The Pharaoh in waiting looked up at him and said, "Of course, you must now leave Thebes, my dear boy. After my grand daughter's, admittedly ill informed objections last night, it is imperative that you go. Were you to remain then it would put our entire project at risk. What do you say Horemheb?"

Without hesitation, the General nodded his complete agreement to Ay's statement and added, "Regrettably, it is for the best. We have done so much now for the good of our country that to fall at the last stage would be criminal. Ankhesenamun will not go along with our plans if Nakht is here. Which territory do you prefer to serve in Commander, Nubia or Syria? The choice is entirely yours."

He spoke as if he was offering the Nakht untold riches, the like of which had never been promised to any man before. Horemheb's tone implied that neither gold, precious gems or turquoise could be compared to this generous offer. Not to mention mere land, preferment and influence. Nakht smiled, as he recognised that he was being stitched up by two consummate experts. Yet again, he had done his job well, but was now going to be sent on his way. There was no real point in arguing with them, as Ay and Horemheb had already decided to move him out of Thebes. They had made up their minds between themselves at his expense. But he decided that this time he would have his say before leaving. As far as Nakht was concerned there would be no more murders on his part. Whether they were done for free or for a promise of non existent rewards. And as for his love of Egypt, last night's ghosts had seen off the last of that sentiment. He had served the state murderously for most of his life. Trying not to shake from his conflicting emotions and the all too evident withdrawal symptoms, he wiped the sweat from his face and said, "Perhaps I might be allowed to take some time off. I could head north and visit what is left of my family in Bathar. You will know where I am, when my services are next required to kill Ankhesenamun…"

"Don't talk like that!" Ay interrupted, angrily, "There will be no more unpleasantness. The killings are finally over and there will be no others. We all have what we want now. Nakht, to be honest with you, I sometimes think that you derive too much enjoyment from your work!"

But before Horemheb could add his sycophantic words of support to the new Pharaoh, Nakht rose to his feet and countered, "You said the word "all". So we are now all supposed to have what we want. Well, you now have the throne Ay. And Horemheb will inherit it from you. But I still have nothing. And this time it is because Ankhesenamun objects to my presence in Thebes. Tell me now Ay, are you ever going to run out of excuses for failing to keep your word? Oh I'm sorry Nakht, I can't give you your reward because the sun will rise tomorrow. Then the High Priest's lowest domestic servant in upper Nubia will start to suspect that you were involved in a conspiracy. So the time is not right and it will never be. Who knows, a river snail might talk to the a member of the Theban priesthood, when he is bathing. And then where would we be? Well, fuck the pair of you. I'm out of it. I've had enough of murdering on demand. So the next time you want somebody to be killed, then you do it yourselves. I'm through with you both!"

In the face of his vehement statement both Ay and Horemheb momentarily hesitated. The dam had burst and twenty nine years of frustration had flowed out in his words. Eventually, the General answered caustically, "You can have your leave of absence. But I suggest that you make it permanent. It does not sit lightly on my shoulders to hear a junior officer talk to his superiors in such an uncouth and bitter manner!"

Nakht was in no mood to be bossed around by Horemheb and retorted, "It would sit even heavier on your shoulders, if I chose to make my involvement in recent events public. Where you two have made your mistake, is that you have always left me with without anything other than platitudes and the ghostly memories of those that I have despatched. After nearly twenty nine years to of service to you Ay, I have nothing to lose. Other than my life, I have no material possessions. So if I feel like making a few public statements on my way back to Bathar, then you must forgive me my indiscretion!"

Ay visibly grimaced at his words before saying, "Perhaps we should not have been so remiss in disregarding your claims. Although if you do challenge the authority of the state, then ultimately you will be the only loser in that game. There are other assassins that we can call upon!"

"Not quite," was Nakht's terse response, "I have already indicated that I can take you both down with me. And that would be before any of your creatures could get to me. As suicidal as that may seem, it is the position that you have forced me into. I am no longer a dog, to be patted on my head and despatched to the furthest extent of our country at your whims. And then recalled to do your bidding, when it suits the pair of you...and without any reward!"

Horemheb, who had been silent for a while stated clearly, "Our Pharaoh is right and you are totally in the wrong. For your information, I could summon the guards now and have you taken away to prison..."

Nakht glared back at him and replied, "And you would be dead a long time before they arrived. Grow up, Horemheb and please stop behaving like a child. A supreme General should at least be capable of acting his age. Can't you see that for once I am being serious? I have already killed two Pharaohs and caused a third to abdicate. To add another and his closest adviser to that number would cause me no greater lack of sleep than I already suffer from."

The Commander of Egypt's mighty armies immediately backed down in the face of Nakht's resolve and wisely chose not to summon the guards. Ay had listened to their conversation carefully and attempted to smooth things over. He smiled and said casually to Nakht, "We should put these differences to one side, especially as the game is already won in our favour. But for the sake of the argument, what would ensure your silent departure and speedy retirement to Bathar?"

"Just what I have been promised many times in the past. Although I know from your self serving justifications, that there is no prospect of those promises being honoured. But let us see what you can offer me. And please don't tell me again how ungrateful I am being. It won't work on this occasion..."

Horemheb opened his mouth and attempted to speak, but Nakht turned upon him menacingly and said, "Only talk when I ask you to open your mouth, lick spittle. Your neck may still snap in my hands, whatever Ay offers me!"

To reinforce his point Nakht rose to his full height and towered over the seated Horemheb. The General was lost for words and avoided meeting the soldier's glance full on. But Ay came to the General's rescue by saying to Nakht, "Let us suppose that you were to retire to the Nile delta. Would a large payment of gold smooth your path and send you on your silent way? I think that I could arrange that quite easily. Naturally, it would be commensurate with your past services and sufficient to ensure you a comfortable return to your old home ground."

Nakht looked at his ageing former patron and answered, "Yes that sounds very acceptable to me. As long as it is forthcoming quickly. As things now stand, I could kill you both and disappear into the countryside without any recriminations. Tomorrow will be quite different. So I suppose that it's your call, Ay."

The new Pharaoh buried his head in his hands for and pondered for a while, before saying reluctantly, "I'm sorry Nakht, but this can't be done right away. And certainly, not before the sun falls. I just don't keep that amount of disposable wealth in my private residence. Just give me twenty four hours to sort it all out. By then you will have enough of the precious metal to last you for the rest of your life. Then you can head north and set yourself up in real style. So let the three of us agree to meet at at breakfast time tomorrow, here at the palace. And this awful unpleasantness between us can be ended amicably, so that we can all move on. Are you in agreement with my proposed course of action Nakht?"

The soldier nodded his assent and prepared himself to leave the room. Mentally, he thought that Ay's throne names would have to include the adjectives mendacious and duplicitous. But keeping such thoughts to himself Nakht said, "I'll see you both at midday tomorrow. And by the way Horemheb, Your wife Mutnodjme, told me your cock is always as flaccid as the baker's floppy dough. But she had no complaints about how stiff my prick was. It seemed to satisfy her well enough. Now I will bid you good day, gentlemen until the same time tomorrow."

Nakht left the two silent and now subdued men together. He went to his guest room and picked up a heavy blanket. Then he walked straight out of Ay's residence, by the back door and headed south. What little money he possessed, the Commander always kept about him in his purse. The former soldier had no intention whatsoever of presenting himself to Ay and Horemheb at the appointed hour on the following day. By then, if not before, they would have an armed force of fifty men present to arrest and kill him. He also had no intention of travelling towards the Nile delta and Bathar. They would find it too easy to locate him there. This was what Nakht had intended, when he had falsely expressed his travel plans. That would be the first place that they tried to track him down. So it was the last place that he intended to visit for a while.

Outside of the new Pharaoh's residence, in the the morning's fresh air, Nakht suddenly felt very good within himself. It had been some time since he had been free of instructions and orders. Not since his childhood in Bathar, twenty nine years ago. Now he would be his own master. There would be no more of Ay's pathetic lies for him to listen to. Not another false promise to hang onto, in the hope of getting the wealth and advancement that he was owed. Or for that matter another person to kill. No more accusatory ghosts to add to those that had started to trouble him. That part of his life was now over. And Horemheb was now out of his life as well. He had also enjoyed speaking his mind to the General. Although Nakht had never fucked Mutnodjme, the seeds of doubt had been sown in the arsehole's mind. Hopefully, they would take root and cause Horemheb some genuine discomfort. He deserved it in Nakht's opinion.

    The western side of Thebes had never looked so good to him, as he swiftly made his way to a river crossing. After taking a ferry across the river to the eastern bank, he sought out a tavern where he was not known. A few fortifying beakers of wine later, Nakht went to the tradesmen's part of the town. There he purchased several sheets of blank papyrus, some black ink and five quill pens. He wrapped them in his blanket and continued to head towards the south on foot, leaving Thebes behind. The soldier had decided to become an itinerant scribe, who was quite prepared to live from hand to mouth. After all, it had been his boyhood ambition and his late father's dream for him as well. Walking from town to town and village to village, along the Nile would provide him with a good living. He was never going to be short of food or beer. And his work should provide him with enough of an income to afford wine when the sun set. Although Nakht intended to keep his distance from the regions' temples. There was no way that he could be sure that the reinstated priests were not in the pay of Ay or Horemheb. Besides, he could now invent his own spells to sell to the ever gullible populace.

Chapter Twenty Two

Nakht's leisurely southern route allowed him to immerse himself completely into the Nile's hinterland. Although his size and shape marked him out from the ordinary Egyptian man, the former soldier took great care to avoid government officials and troops. He was in no doubt that both Horemheb and Ay would be looking for him. By his estimation, his ruse of heading north could only have bought him two weeks at the most. Word of his departure and questions about his whereabouts would have already been sent out, along with the administration's normal communications. But he criss-crossed the Nile on ferries, several times a day, to throw any would be pursuers off his trail. And as he put distance between himself and Thebes, the ex-Commander started to relax. Although his demons did not leave him entirely alone at night, he began to win the battle against his dependency on alcohol.

This had been very hard at first. But Nakht had long realised that excessive drinking had been doing his body great harm. It wasn't pleasant waking up every morning and feeling like shit. And the sweats and the trembling had been getting worse for some considerable time. In his new job of scribing for a living, he could not afford to shake. The villagers could not decipher his hieroglyphs, but they wanted them to look right. So he started to dry himself out, in the course of his travels. At first, it was very agonising for Nakht, as the withdrawal symptoms took immediate effect. His body felt great pain at being denied his daily fix of wine or beer. A whole week passed before his hands were steady enough for him to offer his services to potential customers. In that time he exhausted most of the slender resources that he had brought from Thebes.

The first two days were the worst. Then he was unable to sleep at night, as the moment that his eyes closed Nakht, was instantly jerked back into consciousness.

But after seven days of absolute agony, the pain finally eased. He started to work again and his appetite slowly recovered. And unlike his childhood in Bathar, the demand for his scribing was not only restricted to writing spells. Following the country's recent upheavals, even the peasant farmers wanted long term stability as well as religious sanction from the gods. In their case, it took the form of legal documents which clearly stated their intentions for the disposal of personal property. It presented a very good market to Nakht. There was strong demand for this type of document throughout the southern countryside. He prospered by being able to undercut the rates charged by the local temple's priests or the district administration's officials. Although Egypt had never developed a comprehensive monetary exchange system, payment in kind was always forthcoming. Especially when his customers could scent a bargain. So the former soldier did not go hungry. He also did not go thirsty, but generally avoided wine and restricted himself to the consumption of beer. That was until his journey eventually brought him to Kawa.

At the back of his mind, Nakht had always known that his southerly trek would lead him into Nubia and to the town of Kawa. He had not set off specifically to go there, as his primary aim had been to get away from Ay and Horemheb. But the direction of his journey meant that he at least had to pass through the southern town. By this stage he had been on his travels for almost three months. His personal possessions now included a cloak and a thick blanket, to protect him against the cold night air. So sleeping rough was no great problem, although he found it no great pleasure. Scribing occupied his mind during the day and at night he slept much better than when he had been in Ay's service. Ghostly visits and flashbacks started to diminish. The former soldier recognised that not having to kill anybody, since he had left Thebes was an important factor in this. But as he approached Kawa, his newly found sense of well being started to desert him. It had been over ten years since he had seen Nefertiti and Merytamun. Nakht was not sure of the reception that he would receive from the two women. But he knew inside himself that approaching them was something which he needed to do. Whatever the consequences of the visit turned out to be.

When he arrived in Kawa, the itinerant scribe did not seek the women out immediately. Instead he found some lodgings and set about earning his keep. Just as out in the countryside, there was more than enough work to keep the lions from his door. For more than a week, Nakht worked busily in the market place during the day and at night acquainted himself with the layout of the town. He even visited the temple that Tutankhamun had funded, as the price of Nefertiti's sanctuary. Unfortunately, the familiarisation exercise also involved a lot of time sitting in bars. So he started to drink again. Not heavily at first, but the former soldier noticed that as each day passed, his consumption of alcohol was increasing. He realised that it was time for him to make a move, before he reverted to his painful, chronic state of dependency again.

His reluctance to approach Nefertiti and her daughter in Kawa was not only based upon fears of personal rejection. Nakht was well aware that by now, Ay would be searching the country for him in every direction. It would only be a matter of time before descriptions of a tall and muscular scribe, operating in the far south of Nubia, reached Thebes. Under Akhenaten the country and its territories had become a police state. But neither Ay or Horemheb had shown any inclination to change that in the years following the heretic's death. So although he had found out where the two women lived, just after he had arrived in the southern town, he could not just turn up and make himself known to them. First, he had to check out the level of security that surrounded them. This turned out to be minimal. A single policeman, no doubt detailed by the local administration, stood outside their well appointed residence during the daylight hours. Although Nakht still expected a trap. Both Horemheb and the new Pharaoh were aware of his relationship with Nefertiti. In their place, he would have anticipated his visit to Kawa and made the appropriate arrangements.

But they seemed not to have thought that far ahead. Or maybe ruling Egypt left them little time to devote to Nakht. By the end of his second week in Kawa, Nakht had not noticed any change in the level of protection around Nefertiti's house. He had also not seen either of the women around the town. Their servants were sent out to do the shopping on a daily basis and the house had few visitors. Feeling sure that it was now time to make himself known, the former Commander finished a busy day's work in the market place. He paid off his landlord, telling him that he had to return to the north of the country on family business. This was a standard lie that he used to throw any potential trackers off his trail. Pointing them in the wrong direction would always buy him some time. After making his farewells to the landlord and leaving the lodging house, Nakht made his way through the narrow streets to Nefertiti's home. He waited at the back of the house for several hours until Kawa was quiet. Then he silently forced his way into the building and made his way to the upper part of the house.

Once inside the residence, he climbed to the house's higher levels as silently as he could manage.

The first room that he looked into was dark and empty. By now his eyes had adjusted to the lack of light. In the second room he saw the peacefully sleeping form of Merytamun, who was snoring loudly. Closing her door very gently, he moved towards the upper floor's third room and pulled open the door. It turned out to be Nefertiti's bedroom and she was not asleep. Akhenaten's former Queen was sat up in her bed reading a papyrus script. Like anybody would be, she was initially disturbed at the sight of an unexpected male intruder in her room. But before she decided to shout for help, the size and appearance of Nakht's broad shape registered in her mind. As Nefertiti recognised her former lover, in the glow of the oil light, her fears swiftly turned to amazement and she said in complete disbelief, "You can't be here to kill me. Not after the news that I have recently received from Thebes. So why, in the name of Horus are you here now, at this time of the night?"

Nakht pulled up a chair and sat down at her bedside. Although it had been a very long time since they had been intimate, he could see that she had aged well in the intervening years. But before he could gather together his thoughts and reply Nefertiti continued, "Did my father remove your tongue before your departure from Thebes or have you taken a vow of perpetual silence?"

"Neither," he answered, unable to take his eyes off her smoothly shaved head. Nakht swore to himself that the woman had discovered the secret of eternal youth. She didn't look a day older than when she had been the Pharaoh Smenkhkare. Nefertiti was also looking closely at her former lover. She put her papyrus scroll to one side and said, "It seems as if you have only one word to say to me. Was it really worth your long journey to say that?"

Nakht grinned at her challenge. She had also lost none of her spirit or playfulness. He answered, "I was passing through Kawa and decided to call by..."

"That's nonsense," she interrupted, "You've been sat in the market place for almost two weeks doing your scribing. Don't think that I haven't seen you from a distance!"

Her assertion surprised him. After swallowing heavily he countered, "Well I certainly didn't see you. And I was looking out for you. But tell me what news do you have from Thebes? Since I left your father's service, I am more than a little bit out of touch."

Nefertiti laughed and replied, "And you are more than a little bit out of favour. Horemheb has promised ten pieces of gold for any man that apprehends you. My father has been less generous in posting a smaller reward. But I'm sure you know all about his parsimony. Oh and my daughter Ankesenamun is dead. The unholy duo decided that she had no more use to them, after Ay's coronation. His first wife Tiy is now the Pharaoh's great wife."

"Well I didn't kill her. That part of my life is now finished. Why do you think that I walked out on Ay?"

"Because he never made good on his promises to you. I know well enough what my own father is like. But I don't blame you in any way for being caught up in his schemes. After all, I was too for many years. Though you still haven't told me what you are doing here."

"I just wanted to see you," Nakht answered, sheepishly, "I've always thought that we had unfinished business between ourselves."

Nefertiti nodded and replied, "I swear that you're blushing! But listen to me. I had to end our affair, when you made me pregnant. Although, my father had told me even then that I was going to be the interim

Pharaoh. By that stage it was obvious that my late husband had gone too far with his new religion. So you were removed from Ay's plans, at least where I was concerned. We both followed his instructions, in our own ways...and where has it got us? I'm living in exile and you are on the run. Now, you can stay here tonight, but you'd better leave early in the morning. The administration's spies are everywhere and you have been in Kawa for far too long for your own good. And it's not as if you are a small and unobtrusive figure in this little town..."

As Nefertiti finished talking, she pulled back the bedsheets and indicated to Nakht that he should join her. Once he was inside her bed, they cuddled each other closely and remembered a time when they were both much younger and far more vigorous. They talked about times past and Nefertiti told him about Neferneferure, the daughter Nakht had never known. He told her about the ghosts, the flashbacks and his drinking. And how his proud desire to serve the state had died, due to broken promises and the realisation of his awful crimes.

The following morning, Nakht left the house early some time before Merytamun awoke. Nefertiti was right. He needed to keep moving. Although he had enjoyed the chance to be with her and he did not regret his visit to Kawa. They had not made love, but the short time that they had spent together had been good. It gave him a type of resolution to a part of his life that had been ended prematurely. He had no doubt that news of his two weeks stay in Kawa itself would soon be known in Thebes. So to confuse his anticipated pursuers, he took a ferry across the Nile and started the long walk towards a little known Western desert oasis. He was sure that they wouldn't think to look for him in that part of the country for a while. And when they did, he would have moved on to somewhere else. The former soldier realised that there were no quick fixes or instant solutions to the serious problems that he faced. Just the knowledge that for every day he was able to avoid detection by Ay's or Horemheb's agents he was winning. And they were losing and not sleeping as well as he did at night. Which was all more than enough to keep him going. Fuelled by that thought, his long legs kept a spring in his stride, as he headed across the desert towards to the small oasis settlement.

Conclusion

Nakht continued to weave his way around the countryside, even passing incognito through Thebes on several occasions. His years of military service in Nubia and Syria had honed his survival instincts well. The former soldier always managed to stay at least one step ahead of Ay and Horemheb's spies. As time had passed, he settled into his new life quite well and did not miss his previous existence in the slightest. But being removed from the centres of power also had its disadvantages. Out in the countryside, when he heard about news from Thebes, it was always some time since it had happened. Some two years after his departure, he heard that Horemheb had assumed the co-regency. That was not a surprising development. It had been a part of the deal that the two men had agreed between them, after Tutankhamun's death. Although inside himself, Nakht had always assumed that Ay would have tried to renege on this. From his own experience the Pharaoh was not to be trusted, once his purposes had been served. So it showed him that the general's star had risen back into the ascendancy. Ay must have needed Horemheb more than the younger man needed him. The itinerant scribe considered himself to be well out of it. He had no doubt that his services would have been called on by both men, to resolve their argument.

It was just over two years later that he hear about Ay's death. At the time he was working in the eastern desert, close to Wadi Hammamat. Horemheb was now the sole Pharaoh and totally in charge of Egypt and her colonies. Personally, Nakht did not suspect foul play. After all, the late Pharaoh had been in his mid seventies. And for some years before his own hurried departure from Thebes, the old man had never looked well without his make-up pasted on. So, the former soldier was prepared to rule out foul play on this occasion. But what surprised him was Horemheb's reaction to the old fraud's death. It took some time for Nakht to discover the details, which only emerged gradually. Firstly, the new Pharaoh embarked on a programme of strict reforms to the government's administration. He had decided to root out corruption and inefficiency in both the army and the civil service. There was even talk of a great edict, which listed his intentions, being carved in the temple at Karnak. As Nakht had always failed to benefit materially from his services to Ay, he gave Horemheb's endeavour his silent support. Although, he still recalled that the General had willingly advanced his own early career though Ay's patronage.

But the next stage of the new Pharaoh's direction was amazing to him. At one time, while he was working close to Thebes, wild rumours started to circulate. They stated that Horemheb had personally supervised the desecration of Ay's tomb, in the Valley of the Kings. His predecessor and former friend had suddenly become a non person. The former soldier could easily understand the present King taking Ay's construction works away from the deceased ruler. It was standard practice for Pharaohs to do that to their predecessors and a quick way to proclaim their own greatness. Older cartouches were removed and replaced by the name of the current ruler. Nobody was hurt by this process and it was nowhere near as serious a matter as desecrating a dead man's tomb. Nakht could only assume that Horemheb felt as resentful towards Ay, as he personally had done four years earlier.

The desecration was officially "justified" and sanctioned on the grounds that Ay had been a heretic. Like Akhenaten and Tutankhamun before him, the late Pharaoh was portrayed as a follower of the Aten. Now

Nakht knew this to be totally untrue. In all his experience of the dead ruler, it had been apparent that Ay had never actually believed in the Aten. Ay may have worshipped the solar disc in Armana, but that was only because it was required by Akhenaten. And as a senior courtier he had been left with no choice. At that time, neither Horemheb nor Nakht had a choice either. They had all attended Akhenaten's ceremonies together, when they had been present in the city. The former Commander was unable to recall Horemheb objecting to the worship of Akhenaten's god. But eventually, it dawned upon him that this was all a part of the new Pharaoh's master plan. He obviously wanted to put some distance between himself and his direct predecessors. Egypt's countryside was still in turmoil, to a certain extent. This was despite the fact that though so many years had elapsed since the end of the Armana experiment. On his own travels, Nakht had not suffered personally as a result of this. Although that was primarily because of his imposing stature. Sensibly, very few people that he met wanted to trouble him. But as a result of his own experiences, he had closely observed that civil disobedience was still rife. Horemheb was planning to stamp his authority on Egypt, so that he could rule in a way that had not been seen since Amenhotep III's early years.

    Once Nakht had realised this, he kept an even lower profile than he had done previously. There was still scribing work for him to do, but he barely lingered longer than a day in each village. That was until Horemheb's crackdown eased. Although like the rest of Egypt, he received no official news that this was over. The current government did not operate in such a way. But he knew that when the Pharaoh moved the capital to Memphis his wave of reforms and repressions were over. Just like the Amenhotep III and Akhenaten before him, Horemheb had found the priesthood of Thebes too difficult a nut to crack. Corruption and civil disobedience was easier to deal with by comparison. By this stage, Nakht also suspected that the King barely gave him a moments thought. It was over five years since he had stormed out of Ay's residence. In the intervening years his memory must have dimmed in Horemheb's mind. So after giving the matter much thought, he decided that it was time for him to retire to the Nile Delta.

Nakht was now 46 years old. And after his many years away from the area he had grown up in, he finally felt that it was safe for him to put down some roots and to retire there. Horemheb could get on with the job of being the King. He also hoped Nefertiti would continue to enjoy her retirement in Kawa with her daughter. Nakht looked forward to farming a small plot of land (close to, but not actually in Bathar), fishing the river and doing the odd bit of scribing. It would be his own personal fields of Yaru. But it would be in this life and not the next. Despite his current personal redemption, he knew that there were too many ghosts waiting for him in the afterlife, for it to be a pleasant prospect to face...

Postscript

It is very hard to know where to start with a brief guide to Egyptian history. Even when it relates to a single dynasty of one of the three main Kingdoms. But I want to try and place the story which you have just read into its proper historical context. And that is where the difficulty starts. The New Kingdom started over 1500 years before Christ's birth. So chronology is a constant source of disagreement between students of Egypt's history, as of course is the interpretation of facts. I am quite sure that if any two eminent Egyptologists were placed in a room together, they would argue about dates, but would never actually come to blows about dating Egypt's history. Firstly, because they would be unable to agree that they were actually together, in the room, at the same moment in time. This is because variances in dates for events, such as the start or end of a Pharaoh's reign, can easily be placed as far as thirty years apart by any two authorities. So in a list of reigns and dates of 18th Dynasty Pharaohs, please be aware that all dates are approximate. The second reason why our hypothetical Egyptologists would not come to blows relates to the interpretation of events. As you will see from the details of the characters I used in the novel, this is wide and varied, not to mention often contradictory. So if one historian threw a punch at another, the second could quite easily interpret it as a sign of friendship. Or deny that the punch was ever thrown.

I will start by saying that my main protagonist Nakht, is an imaginary character. But I have found references to three people, who had the same name and lived in the time of the New Kingdom. The first, was a scribe who worked for both Tuthmosis IV and

Amenhotep III. There was also a poor Theban weaver of that name, who lived around the time of the 20th dynasty. And finally, I found a reference to a military officer in the employ of Horemheb, at the time of Armana. I would also like to say that I have used modern names for the locations of this novel. An example of this is Thebes, which is Greek in origin.

With respect to the Pharaohs and their wives. Amenhotep III ruled between BC 1382 and 1344. His great wife was called Queen Tiy. It is probable that he succeeded to the throne as a child. When he died he may have been only forty five years old. As I stated in the story, he is understood to have been a forceful ruler, who consolidated Egypt's wealth by means of international trade. He also had disagreements with the Karnak priesthood, whose influence and wealth were said to rival his own. Indeed, the aspirations of the priesthood to equal or surpass their monarch are based in fact. The White Chapel at Karnak was demolished on his command and used as fill for the building of a great pylon. But the pylon fell down and the fill was excavated in modern times. The excavations revealed a carved image of the first priest having equal precedence with the Pharaoh in front of Amun-Re. That was on a par with treason and heresy in Ancient Egypt.

It is believed, but disputed by some, that Amenhotep's mummy was found in the Valley of the Kings in tomb KV35. A medical examination showed the corpse to have been suffering from chronic mouth disorders. This gave rise to the view that he spent the last few years of his life, dosed up with wine and the essence of blue lotus, to ease his insufferable pain. It is not impossible to believe this, as Amenhotep III had a reputation for enjoying food and drink to his utmost capabilities, during much of his life.

Amenhotep IV or Akhenaten, succeeded his father and reigned from BC 1352 to 1336. Straight away you can see the difficulty with dates. Amenhotep III died in BC 1344, eight years after his son took the throne. But allowing for his father's poor health and the system of co-regency the dates are still possible. His great wife was originally known as Nefertiti, but under the new religion she was renamed Nefer-Nefru-Aten. She is believed to be Ay's daughter, although some Egyptologists claim that she was a foreign princess. Akhenaten is credited, or blamed, for introducing our world's first monotheistic religion. However, certain authorities dispute that the worship of the Aten was entirely monotheistic. But he did move the capital and people from Thebes to a new city in the desert called Armana. This is yet more evidence of his struggle with the Theban priesthood. Firstly, a new religion is introduced, with the Pharaoh as its only priest. Secondly, the power base of the administration is moved many miles away. He had a favourite minor wife, called Kiya, who is thought to be the mother of Tutankhamun. She is referred to in texts as a greatly beloved wife. Nefertiti disappears from the historical records after the twelfth and most glorious year of his reign. Akhenaten also married three of his daughters, one of whom Mekytaten died in childbirth. There is a great debate as to whether he suffered from Marfan's syndrome (a genetic disorder), which is ongoing. It is accepted that he died during the seventeenth year of his reign, possibly in suspicious circumstances.

The question of what happened to Nefertiti is fascinating. Until her disappearance all the surviving carvings and images, show her enjoying an idyllic lifestyle. There are pictures of a loving husband, together with his wife and children, below the rays of the Aten. And then she vanishes from the pages of

Egyptian history. It is possible that she had died, as remnants of an Ushabti funerary statue, inscribed with her name, have been found at Armana. These are now to be found in a museum in Berlin. It is also suspected that Nefertiti may have been disgraced. Her name was replaced, on inscriptions, which then showed her daughter Merytaten as the King's great wife. But there is another possibility, namely that she became Smenkhkare, the Pharaoh who ruled between BC 1336 and 1334. That theory has several proponents, although it is hotly disputed. If it were true, then she would have to had married her daughter Merytaten. She is listed as the great Queen for that short reign. Indeed, some Egyptologists believe that Merytaten or her new Hittite husband was actually Smenkhkhare. But to be a female Pharaoh in the New Kingdom was not impossible and unknown. It had been happened 100 years earlier with Hatshepsut. And even earlier, in the 6th dynasty, a female called Neitiqerty may have had ruled Egypt. Of course, it would happen again in the Ptolemy dynasty with Cleopatra.

    The reign of Tutankhamun followed, from BC 1334 to 1325. I think that most Egyptologists would agree with the contention that the word "reign" is used very loosely. The young Pharaoh was only seven when he ascended to the throne. His mummy indicates that he was no more than seventeen when he died. Although, true to form, even that age is disputed by a year or two! But what cannot be refuted is that he was a child ruler and directly influenced by two powerful historical figures – Ay and Horemheb. There were other influences, such as his wife Ankesenamun and the courtier Tutu. The former, was older than her husband by some five years. Ankhesenpaaten, as she was known, at the time of her marriage to Tutankhamun, had already given birth to a child by her father Akhenaten. So she must at least have passed the age of puberty, before she married the younger Tutankhamun. Tutu's existence is fairly well documented, although some sources say that he was called Dudu. It is understood that he was of foreign birth from Palestine and there is evidence to show his self serving treachery.

The circumstances of Tutankhamun's death are confusing, but less so than the death of his father. It is worth reminding ourselves that many Pharaohs were buried in the Valley of the Kings. But his is the only mummy to remain in its burial place to this day. Because of this undisputed fact forensic examinations have been possible. Thirty years ago, x-rays of his body were taken in Liverpool. When they were examined by specialists, an area of bone damage was discovered at the base of his skull. The medical opinion went as far as to stress that this was evidence of a fatal blow. But not an instantly terminal wound. As the x-rays showed signs of bone regrowth, it was likely that Tutankhamun had spent several months in a coma. So it seems likely that the young King was murdered.

Of course, this is the subject of much debate. There is a school of thought that dismisses such an interpretation. But disregarding those objections, there are three main suspects; Ay, Horemheb and Ankesenamun. As the young man was approaching an age when he could think and act for himself, either of the three could have had a motive. Ay, who was over seventy years of age, could have seen the Kingship slipping away from him. The army's supreme General Horemheb was afraid of the young Pharaoh's ineffectual rule in the face of continued Hittite incursions. And Ankesenamun may have wanted the throne for herself. But, as always with Egyptian history, there is at least one other possibility. Officially, both Ay and Horemheb put themselves in the clear. They placed any blame firmly on the shoulders of Tutu through the statements of the priesthood.

Ay succeeded Tutankhamun as Pharaoh and ruled from BC 1325 to 1321. Evidence was found in the 1920s to indicate that he married Ankhesenamun. An ancient ring with their cartouches inscribed together, side by side, was discovered. This was only normally done to celebrate a royal wedding. As Ay is thought to have been Nefertiti's father, it would appear that he married his own granddaughter. So if Tutankhamun was murdered, it is not impossible to believe that his direct successor had the most to gain. Ay's existence is well documented, apart from the evidence of his tomb, he was known to be Master of Horses for Akhenaten. Later he became Vizier and Chancellor to the ruler. It is also thought that he was the brother in law of Amenhotep III, making the confusing family relationships even more confused. But what is indisputable about his reign is that it did not last for long before General Horemheb came to the throne.

But before we look at Horemheb's reign, it is necessary to consider Ankhesenamun. To place ourselves in her shoes, we must think about a young woman who was married three times. Her father was her first husband and her half brother was her second. She was then faced with the prospect of marrying her own grandfather. Perhaps it is no surprise that she wrote to the Hittite King Suppiluliumas asking for a new husband, of royal blood. Maybe she thought that she could outwit Ay. Or more likely she wanted to avoid an early death. Either way she was not successful. Her Hittite prince was murdered and shortly after she disappeared from history. All the images from Ay's reign show his wife Tiy as the King's great wife. Ankhesenamun's fate can only be considered to be a matter of unpleasant and sad speculation.

Horemheb succeeded Ay and ruled from BC 1323 to 1295. He was the last King of the 18th dynasty. The General was the logical successor, as Ay died without an heir. Following his accession there was a crack down, in an attempt to restore law and order. Ay's tomb in the Valley of the Kings was desecrated and the former Pharaoh portrayed as a heretic. But Horemheb also tried to root out and punish corruption inherent in the administration. His "Great Edict", which was inscribed on the 10th Pylon at Karnak is proof of this and the text exists to this this day. Like all Pharaohs of the 18th dynasty he embarked on a programme of building works. Although this did not preclude him from claiming Tutankhamun's and Ay's works as his own. Horemheb died without an heir and nominated another military man to be his successor. That was Rameses I, the first King of the 19th dynasty.

I mentioned at the start of this postscript that dates and interpretation were open to opinion. Interpretation of events will always depend upon a person's views and beliefs. There is no way that will ever be uniform. The chronology of the 18th dynasty is also wide open to interpretation. Over 3500 years have elapsed since the reign of Amose I, the first ruler of the 18th dynasty. Obviously, the passage of time does not make the chronology easier to define. It is made more difficult by the the desecration which followed the end of the Armana experiment. The Egyptians were great list keepers both of the trivial and the important. Lists of their Pharaohs were maintained at the major temple sites. But the Armana Kings were erased from the lists. Their cartouches were chiselled from the walls and their existence denied. Which is why Tutankhamun's hurriedly arranged tomb was never discovered until 1922. Egypt and its tomb robbers simply forgot, or never knew, that he had ever existed.

Andrew Drummond, September 2013.

email: ktwc999@gmail.com

Printed in Great Britain
by Amazon